THE KILLER AT LAST!

At the sound of the first shot, Marsh came to his feet. "That ain't no thunderclap," he said.

"No, sir. That's a shot."

The follow-up shots confirmed what Marsh had already suspected. "No hunter is out in the midst of a rainstorm. And that pattern of shooting . . ."

"A gunfight," Serandon said.

"That's right."

"Kidd."

"Very likely."

"So what do we do?"

Marsh did not have time to answer. He was already heading out of the cavern into the rain, his hand wrapped around the cylinder of his unusual rifle to keep it as dry as he could.

HENRY KIDD, OUTLAW

WILL CADE

LEISURE BOOKS NEW YORK CITY

A LEISURE BOOK®

March 2003

Published by

Dorchester Publishing Co., Inc.
276 Fifth Avenue
New York, NY 10001

ISBN: 0-8439-5089-7

Visit us on the web at www.dorchesterpub.com.

HENRY
KIDD,
OUTLAW

CHAPTER ONE

Lightning seared through the sky, silhouetting the abandoned water tank on its teetering tower, illuminating the barren, water-swept main street of what once had been a town. The young mountaineer, far from his home and his element, saw by the lightning's flaring light the broad flatlands, the chaparral blown flat by the wind, the wind-whipped river, the horizon far more distant than any the cloistering mountains of his childhood years had ever allowed him to glimpse.

He saw it all, but scarcely noticed it. His attention was on the dark, lean rifleman who darted across the muddy street, headed for the cover of a narrow alleyway between empty buildings.

Oblivious to the rain that buffeted him on this

dark Texas afternoon, Marsh Perkins left his own refuge behind a rotting pile of ancient firewood and mounted the boardwalk in front of the vacant saloon. He ran down the creaking porch, heading for an alleyway of his own, when the rifleman fired off a shot that smacked into the wall just beside him. By reflex he lunged to the right, through the gaping and glassless front window of the abandoned saloon.

He hit the floor hard and felt its rotting wood yield beneath him. Marsh plunged through splinters and grit to the cool, dank ground below.

The wind knocked out of him, he lay there unmoving for a few moments, stunned at first, then realizing that fate had—perhaps—just done him a favor. He crabbed forward, looking out through a gap in the crumbling foundation. More lightning. The rifleman was there, not fully visible, peering every few moments around the edge of one of the buildings siding the alleyway.

Marsh checked his rifle—an unusual weapon with a revolving cylinder like that of a pistol—and quickly reloaded the three cylinders he had already emptied in this gun battle. Working his way closer to the opening in the foundation, he looked out again, positioned himself as comfortably as possible, and nestled the familiar butt of the rifle against his shoulder.

He took aim at the place where the outlaw Henry Kidd had last thrust out his head. "Go ahead, Kidd," Marsh whispered through gritted teeth. "Get curious. Wonder where I am. Stick that head out one more time and take a look."

The moment he did, Marsh Perkins would be ready. He would fire the shot that would end Henry Kidd's life and bring to an end at last the long quest that had led him to this remote part of Texas all the way from the mountains of western North Carolina. It would be over, thank God, and he would be able to go home and report that he had done what he'd been sent to do.

There it was, the quick look, the head popping out from around the edge of the building just like the turkey heads that Marsh used to shoot off back in Carolina at turkey-shoot competitions down near the trading post. Turkey behind a log, corn scattered at its feet, head bobbing up and down, up and down . . . Turkey shooting was a matter of timing. Of being ready, of sensing when and where that head would next appear . . .

Henry Kidd bobbed his head out, then quickly withdrew it again. Marsh had missed his chance. He gnawed at his lower lip, disappointed. A trickle of mixed sweat and rainwater dripped from one eyebrow, stinging his eyes. He kept ready, kept his aim steady, waiting for that next glance around the corner. Henry Kidd's last look at the world.

It came. Marsh was ready. The finger squeezed, the pistol-style cylinder in the rifle revolved, the hammer fell . . .

A dead click.

For the first time in Marsh Perkins's experience, the rifle given to him by his grandfather, a rifle the old man pried from the clutching fingers of a dead reb bushwhacker, failed him. He couldn't believe it. He pushed the rifle away, glaring at it in disbelief.

Quickly, though, he turned his attention again to the alleyway in which his nemesis hid. The next cylinder would not misfire. He settled the rifle against his shoulder again, squinting down the barrel, aiming at the precise spot from which Kidd had been looking out.

Lightning, more wind, a harder surge of rain . . . but no Henry Kidd. Had he moved?

There he was, darting out and across the street. This move was unanticipated; Marsh wasn't ready for it. He again missed his chance to get off a shot.

Thunder rumbled across the flatlands. Magnificent, deep thunder . . . but when it had rolled off into the distance, Marsh detected another kind of rumble, coming from the earth itself. What the devil? Then he knew. Horses, many of them, coming in a hard rush.

The rumble grew louder. They passed. Marsh saw the blur of their mud-slinging hooves as they passed the front of the old saloon that hid him. He heard voices, shouts, then the hammering percussion of rifles blasting.

"Got him!" someone yelled. "We've killed Henry Kidd!"

Marsh went weak. Kidd was dead?

Who were these men who had just done his work for him?

He felt a draining mix of relief that at last the quest was over, but disappointment that it had been others who brought it to an end. He had traveled many miles and endured many hardships to bring down Henry Kidd, and it seemed unjust that any but him should end Kidd's life. In fact, he'd always believed, based on something told him by his grandmother, that it was actually his personal destiny to be Kidd's destroyer.

He crabbed forward again, working his way out of the gap in the foundation. He tried to make little noise, because he didn't want to startle this band of armed strangers.

Just in case, he lifted his rifle high above his head as he walked toward the riders. He counted ten of them, several now dismounted and gathered around the body of the man Marsh had tracked for so long.

When they detected Marsh's approach, a couple of men reacted quickly by leveling weapons at him. Marsh just kept on approaching, though, his rifle held aloft to show he was not going to use it.

"Who are you?" one of the riflemen yelled in a threatening tone.

"Marsh Perkins, out of North Carolina!" he called back. "I heard someone say Henry Kidd is dead. Is it true?"

"He's deader than stone," someone said.

"Look at him . . . just a rawboned kid," another said, and Marsh couldn't tell if he was talking about him or Kidd. The description would fit in either case. Both he and Kidd had the boyish kind of look that made them seem ten years younger than they were.

"What are you doing here, boy?" the first man demanded. All this gang of strangers was looking at him now.

"I was shooting it out with Henry Kidd before you rode in," Marsh said. "I've been tracking him for months now. I come plumb out of North Carolina to get him."

"Carolina!"

"That's right."

"How do we know you ain't a partner of Kidd?" another man challenged.

"You don't," Marsh replied. "That's why I'm handing you this rifle." He turned his rifle over to the man, who inspected it.

"I ain't seen one of these in years!" he said.

"My grandpap gave it to me and told me to kill Henry Kidd with it," Marsh said.

"You've missed your chance, boy," a man said, and the others chuckled.

Marsh went to the dead man's body, which lay prone on the ground. He rolled it over with his foot. The face was muddied, but the rain washed it away in moments.

"No, I ain't," he replied. "I don't know who his is, but it sure as the devil ain't Henry Kidd."

CHAPTER TWO

A hulking fellow in a big coat eased out of his saddle and walked heavily over to Marsh's side. He had a gray, wide mustache and small eyes. He'd not said a word so far.

He spoke now. "You sure about that, boy?"

"I'm sure," Marsh replied. "I can see how anyone might think this was Kidd from a distance. Same build and general look. But it ain't Henry Kidd."

"Then we've been mightily fooled."

"No more than me. I thought it was Kidd, too. If I'd been closer, I'd have been able to see it wasn't."

"My name's Campbell. Andrew Campbell. I'm the sheriff here," the big man said. "You say your name is Perkins?"

"That's right, sir. Marshall Perkins. Most call me Marsh for short."

"And you've been trailing Henry Kidd all the way out of North Carolina?"

"I can't say I really started trailing him until I got to Texas. But I came to Texas to find him and kill him, so in that sense, yes, I've been tracking him all the way from Carolina."

"Why?"

"He murdered three men and a woman back in Carolina, where I live. Killed them and mangled them up just for meanness. One was my father."

"When was this?"

"Back during the war."

"What? You been tracking Kidd for a decade?"

"No, sir. Just the last six months or so, since I've been able to pick up his track."

The sheriff evaluated Marsh for a few moments. One of the other men nudged at the dead man with his foot and said, "Maybe this ain't Henry Kidd, but it sure as hell is the man who killed Rogers."

The sheriff said to Marsh, "Sounds like you've got a story to tell. I want to hear it. I'm requesting that you come back with me to my office and tell it, once we deal with this dead man here." Then he turned to the man who had just spoken. "Yes, this is the man who killed Rogers. We were just wrong about it being Henry Kidd."

"There's been a murder, then?" Marsh asked.

"Yes. An old man, used to be a dentist until

his fingers got all stiff and sore in the joints and he couldn't work no more. He was robbed and murdered by this fellow on the ground here. We got a posse together, sniffed out his track, and trailed him here to the ghost town. Looks like you were ahead of us."

"I thought it was Kidd," Marsh said. "He's around here, somewhere. I know it for a fact, because I've tracked him for eighty miles. I reckon I've lost the track now, though. This dead man here led me astray."

"You're right. Kidd is in the area. I got a wire out of Hooper County saying he was believed to be coming this way. That's why we believed it was Kidd who killed Rogers. You're certain this ain't Henry Kidd?"

"I'm certain."

"I'll need you to fill out an affidavit to that effect, and sign it. You read and write?"

Marsh Perkins stood up a little straighter. He was literate, one of the few who were in his remote mountain home in an obscure part of western North Carolina. "I can, sir."

"Good. Well, gents, let's gather up this dead man and get him back into town. Maybe somebody will be able to figure out who he is."

"Even if it ain't Kidd, it's a good thing we got him," one of the others said.

"It is," the sheriff said.

"But it means Henry Kidd is still out there," Marsh said. "And that's real bad."

"I can't argue with that," Andrew Campbell said. "Henry Kidd alive means other people dead. And it's meant that for way too long."

"It'll end once I finally get hold of him," Marsh said.

"You speak with confidence."

"It's from being a Perkins. A Perkins is always confident. Especially when it comes to hunting."

"Manhunting included, eh?"

"Especially manhunting."

The lawman nodded. "Let's you and me go talk some."

"Let's do," Marsh replied.

CHAPTER THREE

The dead man was on the slab at the local undertaker's office, coffee bubbled on the stove in the sheriff's office, rain pattered on the roof, and Marsh Perkins sat on a chair with Campbell as his enthralled audience.

He had just signed the affidavit vowing that he knew the face and general appearance of Henry Kidd and that the man killed by the sheriff's posse was not said Henry Kidd. Now the affidavit was laid aside and Campbell leaned across his desk, lower lip sagging as he listened and occasionally responded to Marsh's tale.

"Let me understand this," he said. "Kidd actually cut the dead man's face after he killed him?"

"Into a kind of smile, that's right," Marsh said. "Cut away the flesh of his jaws so that the

11

hole angled up like this." He ran a finger along the side of his face. "Then he dumped the corpse in the midst of the road, so that we can would find it. He wrote his name on him in blood. 'Henry Kidd,' just like he usually does."

"Why'd he kill him?"

"Because my father had refused to give him an old saddle. Kidd demanded it. No right to it, no grounds for claiming it, but he demanded it. It wasn't my father's, though, just on loan to him, so he couldn't give it away even if he wanted. We later figured that he made the demand just so he would get turned down, and have a reason to kill him. Not that Kidd needs a reason."

"He does it for pleasure, from all I hear," the sheriff said. "I've heard of people like that, but never until now have I brushed up this close to a real live one."

"My father was a good man. A churchgoer who'd do no wrong to nobody. He'd even tried to stay clear of the war, because he had folks on both sides and couldn't bear to go against none of them. But Henry Kidd wouldn't bear a man like that to live. Had to kill him."

"How'd Kidd come to be in North Carolina? Born there?"

"Ain't nobody knows. If he was born there, it wasn't in the same parts as me. He just showed up in the mountain country one day, him and some other bushwhacking types. No more than bandits and killers, really. The war meant nothing to them except as an excuse to kill."

"The others he murdered . . . he mangled them too?"

"He always mangles them he kills. At least when he has the chance. He's a man with a demon in him, my grandmammy always said. A man with a demon in him. I believe it. I've never run across so wicked a human being."

"You couldn't have been more than a boy when all this happened. You look to be little more than a boy right now, to be honest."

"I look young. Always have. Baby-faced, they call it. Baby-faced Marsh. I used to fight boys who called me that."

"So how old are you?"

"Twenty-four years old."

"I'd put you at seventeen, not a day more."

"I'm twenty-four. I'll vow it on a Bible."

"About Kidd's age?"

"I'm about four, five years younger than Kidd, I figure it. I was fourteen, maybe fifteen when Kidd did his murders in Carolina."

"I don't understand this. Henry Kidd shows up, murders folks in your neighborhood, and then, a full ten years later, you get sent after him by . . . by who?"

"By my grandmother, most directly. By the community as a whole, really. They picked me to do the job that needs doing."

"Why you?"

"Because I'm the best tracker and hunter that ever come out of the Stone Creek valley. And because back during the war, me and my uncle, Harve Jonely, tracked down a horse thief who'd beat a farmer nigh to death. I was the one who found his trail, and when he shot Uncle Harve out of hiding and left him wounded, it was me who tracked him up a steep ridge with the sun already setting . . . and brought him back."

"Dead or alive?"

"Dead."

"You were a tough and hard young man."

"I was what I had to be. I was what the mountain made me and what the war made me. I still am."

"So this quest for Henry Kidd . . . how exactly did it come about, and why did you wait a full decade to do it?"

"From the day Henry Kidd vanished from the mountains, my granny had it in mind that someday one of her men would find him and avenge them he'd murdered. She had a vision of it . . . things like that happen with her. But she always thought it would be my pap who did it. Not me."

"Why not your uncle?"

"He died. His heart. He wasn't an old man, but it failed him, like it says in the Bible. Young men's hearts failing them. You probably know that verse."

"I don't go to church as much as I should, to tell the truth."

"Well, Pap died, and it fell to me to be the one to go after Henry Kidd . . . but there was no sign of him. No way to know if he was even still among the living. Until that newspaper I showed you arrived."

The sheriff reached to his desk and picked up a crumpled, yellow newspaper page that Marsh had shown him earlier. It was a Texas paper, a small-towner, mostly news reprinted from the bigger papers from San Antonio and Dallas. But there was one item, the story of a murder in which the victim had been left mangled. The murderer was gone, but it was thought, according to the paper, that it was a drifter named Henry Kidd."

"How'd this newspaper get back to North Carolina?"

"It was mailed there. A man who'd grown up on Stone Creek and lived there through the war sent it to my granny. He'd come to Texas after the war, wanting to be a cattleman. He saw the story, remembered. He mailed the newspaper back because he knew we'd need to know."

"And so now you're here."

"Yes."

"How'd you have the traveling money?"

Marsh hesitated at this point. To answer that question fully was something he naturally balked at doing, because it involved a secret that was kept among the mountain folks. But here, miles away in Texas, it probably didn't matter. He cleared his throat and, for the first time in his long journey, revealed to another person the source of his quest's backing.

"Old Sam Bird. He's a Cherokee who's lived up in the mountains above Stone Creek for as long as the mountains have been there . . . or so it seems, anyway. Everybody knows that old

Sam has a mine. The purest silver, Cherokee silver. See the sight on this rifle? That's some of it. He mounted that sight for me, told me it would bring me good luck. But the main thing he did for me was to give me coin."

"Counterfeit?"

"I guess so, in one way of looking at it. But purer silver than anything the government ever pressed out. That's how he's got by with it. His money is worth more than its face value, so nobody who has it gets hurt."

"You got a coin of it on you?"

Marsh reached into his vest pocket and pulled out a rough-edged silver disk and plopped it down before the sheriff.

"There's one. I don't carry many of them. Most of them are in a bank. Anytime I need to, I just send a telegram and they'll do something or other to get money to me. I don't know just how it works, because I ain't had to do it."

"So you're a wealthy man."

"No. Just fixed well enough to keep going for as long as it takes to find Henry Kidd."

"But you ain't found him yet."

"I've come close."

"When you came to Texas, where did you go?"

"Looking for the man who'd sent the newspaper. And I found him. I said a prayer for him by his grave."

"Kidd?"

"That's right. They said he'd gone after Kidd himself. Found his track, and decided to take care of the job himself. Henry Kidd left him hanging upside down by one foot with his throat cut. The name 'Henry Kidd' carved into his forehead. So they told me."

"And Kidd himself was gone."

"Like always. He kills and vanishes. Nobody can catch him—not lawmen, not posses. The army went after him one time. But he just disappears. Like a ghost."

"Or a devil."

"He's worse than the devil."

"You know, son, it's probably not right for me to sit here and tell you that you're doing the right thing. The law ain't something a man should take into his own hands."

"I'm not taking the law into my own hands. Henry Kidd's a wanted man."

"There's a reward, that's true."

"The only reward I want is to take his right hand back to my granny. There's a scar on it, they say, that marks him like a brand. She wants to see it and know he's dead."

"I've heard about that scar. A circle with a kind of slash through it."

"I need to tell you something, Marsh. A man who kills like Kidd kills draws attention. There's plenty of others after him now. Sooner or later, one will get him, especially since there's a reward. It may not be you."

"It'll be me."

"How can you be sure?"

"My granny. She saw it in a vision."

The sheriff toyed with the silver coin again,

watching it glint in the light of the lamp, then handed it back to Marsh. "I like you, son, though you frighten me a bit. I'm always frightened by men who are obsessed with something, even something so righteous as bringing down Henry Kidd.

"Make me one promise: When you do what you have to do, stay on the right side of the law. Watch out that going after a devil don't turn you into a devil yourself."

Marsh dropped the coin into his pocket. "I'll remember that, Sheriff. I will."

CHAPTER FOUR

It would not be hard to remember. From what he knew about Henry Kidd, Marsh had nothing but loathing for the man Kidd was. Robbery Marsh could understand, if the robber was desperate and in true need. Even killing could be abided if a man did it in self-defense. But the kind of crimes Kidd committed often had no secondary motives and seemed to be done for their own sake. They were foul, wicked. Cruel. More than anything else, cruel.

The hotel in this Texas backwater was nothing to grow excited over. Most of it was on one floor, a long, low structure reminiscent of many Mexican dwellings, but over part there was a second story. The man behind the counter was a mix of Anglo and Mexican.

"Room for you?" he asked Marsh in heavily accented English.

"Yes. *Sí.*"

"You are in luck . . . business is slow," the man said, grinning with a flash of gleaming yellow.

"Sorry to hear it."

"It was a joke. Business is always slow," the man explained.

"Oh." Marsh could have figured as much.

"Except for when cowboys come through, looking for women of sport. You like women of sport, *sí*?"

"I always steer clear of them," he said.

"Maria you'd not steer clear of. Maria is a beauty. I'll send her by, no?"

"No."

"You should see her before you say that."

"Is every hotel in Texas a whore parlor?" Marsh had experienced something almost exactly like this in two other locations.

"Not every one. Just the best ones."

"Don't send anybody by my room. Not Maria, not anybody. I want to be left alone."

The man looked disappointed and shook his head subtly. Marsh wondered how much of Maria's earnings he took for his referral services.

Supper was taken in a small cafe down the street. Steak, eggs, and biscuits, the latter soaked in good gravy thickened with flour and served well-peppered. It was late for coffee, but Marsh had three cups anyway because he craved it. And he needed its mind-sharpening effects to help him plan his next move.

How could he track Kidd now? The trail had been broken. He could have cursed himself for letting himself get off onto the trail of the wrong killer. What were the odds that two young murderers of similar physical appearance would be in the same area at roughly the same time? But it had happened, and now Kidd was out there somewhere, and Marsh had no way to track him down.

He ate a piece of rhubarb pie for dessert, making it all the better by having sugared cream poured over it, and finished off his coffee. He paid with coins—not the silver coins he'd brought from home, but with currency he'd traded them for at a bank three or four towns back. He realized how fortunate he was, having resources to travel without having to odd-job his way along.

But self-sufficiency had a price. As it was, depending on no one, he was always alone. Following the bloody trail of a moving murderer, he had little cause to stay long in one place. With no work to do, his contact with other good people was minimal and short-lived. He was left to live with thoughts of little but where Kidd was, where Kidd was going, what Kidd would do next . . . and where the next mangled body would be found.

It was depressing. He longed for it to be over so he could return home, his promise fulfilled, and have a bit of peace again, and think of something besides the devilish young murderer who obsessed him.

In an odd, twisted way, Marsh had developed a sort of admiration for Kidd. Not for what he did—he loathed that—but for his ability to do it without ever being caught. It was downright astonishing that a man could commit the kinds of crimes Kidd did and get away every time. Posse after posse had pursued him, lawman after lawman had sworn to get him. None had.

A few had wound up dead for their efforts. There was a terrible story out of Arkansas about a county marshal who left town to find and kill Henry Kidd—and came back in dragging on the ground behind his own horse, his foot tied to the stirrup and most of his face cut away. They said the man's own mother was the first to see him making his last homecoming.

Marsh wasn't sure he believed the story. Kidd's crimes were so horrific that it was inevitable that legend would grow up around him. Some said he'd killed twenty people over the last two years; Marsh had it figured at more like ten, maybe twelve.

But you never could be sure. An active killer like Kidd might have victims no one even knew about, drifters who could die and be missed by no one. And Kidd required no reason to kill. He did it for its own sake, whenever the mood struck him. Who could say who might have died by his hand in places where the crime would never be detected?

Marsh in some ways knew Henry Kidd better

than any other man, though he'd never truly met him, not in the face-to-face, words-sharing kind of way. He'd seen him twice from a distance, for certain, and one other time closer at hand . . . not so certain. It might have been another case of mistaken identity, like today.

He wondered sometimes if Henry Kidd had seen him in turn, and would remember his face whenever the day came that Marsh put a bullet through his heart.

If Kidd knew, somehow, that Marsh was following him, Marsh figured Kidd was more flattered than worried. Henry Kidd was proud of his sinful work. Only a proud man would do what Kidd did to his dead victims, only a man struttingly pleased with his own wickedness.

With his belly full almost to discomfort, Marsh walked the dark streets of the town. He wasn't tired enough to go to bed or willing to endure the boredom of sitting still.

His horse was in the livery, his weapons locked in his hotel room, except for the one small pistol he wore beneath his coat, a hideout gun that he carried in violation of the laws of most towns, probably this one included. He didn't worry about it. Most men carried guns somewhere on their person, and it wasn't an issue unless a show was made of it. Marsh couldn't afford to be unarmed when his quarry was one such as Kidd. There was always that chance of rounding a corner and encountering Kidd. Should that ever happen, Marsh did not intend to be unarmed.

*   *   *

He detected the man behind him as he turned a corner. Big fellow, broad, yellowish hat that was much battered and greased, clothing that was dusty from the trail so that the color was hard to make out. Though he moved in shadows, it appeared that his hair was sandy, nearly blond. He wore a mackinaw and boots; no more details than that could Marsh make out.

Marsh made no show of having seen the man, but walked nonchalantly along the boardwalk onto which he'd just turned, and ducked into the first alley after the next turn. When the man passed, looking here and there in an uncertain way, Marsh stepped out and gripped his shoulder, pulling him around to face him.

CHAPTER FIVE

The man almost jumped out of his boots. "What the—"

"You looking for me?"

The man, who had a ruddy face and eyebrows that were so light they blended right in with his skin, was speechless a few moments, then burst out laughing. This surprised Marsh, to say the least, and he actually took a step back and began to slowly reach for his pistol.

"Something funny?" he said.

"Nothing but myself . . . What a fool I am, to let myself be outsmarted by a boy!"

The accent was nothing American, but subtle and hard to place.

"I'm no boy. Haven't been for years."

"Well, you look it. You look like you've still got mama's milk on your lip there. Or might that be the start of a wispy mustache?"

Marsh could tell he didn't like this fellow. Anyone that would trail a stranger in a strange town, then mock him to his face, was unusual if nothing else.

"I do believe it's a mustache," said a voice from behind. Marsh turned and saw another man, similar in size, coloration, and accent to the first. He'd approached while Marsh was preoccupied with the first fellow. "No lap child, this one, though he may look it."

"Who are you men and why were you following me?" Marsh demanded.

The first man laughed again and stuck out a big hand. Marsh wasn't inclined to take it, and didn't, for fear the man would yank and restrain him while the other pilfered his pockets.

"Very well, then," the man said, lowering his hand and remaining as jovial as ever. "I suppose a man is right to be wary of strangers. So I'll make us strangers no longer. My name is Knutsen. Rolph Knutsen. This is my brother, York."

"Pleased to meet you, young manhunter," York said.

Manhunter? What was this all about?

"I'd say I was pleased, too, except I don't know why you were following me."

"Simply wanted to meet you, that's all. We have something in common, you and us," Rolph said.

"We're on the track of Henry Kidd," York said.

Marsh eyed them cautiously. "Bounty hunters?"

"Indeed. There are sizable rewards being posted for bringing in Henry Kidd, both private and public. We intend to claim them all," said Rolph.

"Too bad for you, I'm afraid," York said condescendingly. "We heard it told of you that you've trailed him all the way from the East."

"Who's been talking about me?"

"There's a deputy sheriff here who loves to drink, and when he drinks, he tells what he's overheard young manhunters saying to the local sheriff."

From the smell of York's breath, Marsh surmised he enjoyed drinking, too.

"That's right," Rolph threw in. "He tells us all about this eager boy manhunter from the East who says he's trailing Henry Kidd, and about how this boy manhunter nigh got himself killed today trying to do what should be left to grown-up men . . . and it ends up the man he thinks is Henry Kidd isn't Henry Kidd at all! So York and I look at one another, and decide we need to meet this boy manhunter, and tell him to go back east and leave the tracking to men who know what they are doing."

"Yeah," said York, though it sounded more like "Ya."

Marsh looked at the brothers. "Well, gentlemen, I have to disappoint you, because I can't back off from what I'm doing. I've gone too many miles to quit now. And I made a promise

27

that I'd bring back Henry Kidd's scarred hand to show that those he'd murdered back home have been avenged."

The brothers glanced at each other and laughed. "You're going to cut off his hand?"

"That's right. I'll cut it off, pack it in salt, and take it back to North Carolina."

They laughed again. "You should be in dime novels," Rolph said.

"Ya," York chimed in. "They could call it 'The Boy Manhunter Who Went After Henry Kidd's Hand and Got Killed.' " They roared. This apparently was high humor in their book. Marsh stared at them, not even blinking.

The laughter died, and Rolph suddenly was serious. He thumped a forefinger on Marsh's chest. "Listen to me, boy manhunter. That reward is ours. You nor anyone else will get it."

"Ya," York said.

"I'm not after reward," Marsh replied. "I just want Henry Kidd."

The brothers laughed again. Rolph had a touch of alcohol on his breath, too, Marsh detected. He wasn't sure what was funny about what he'd just said.

"You let it go, boy. Get back home to your mother," Rolph said.

"Ya," said York. "We're the ones who have the track now. Not you. Go home or we'll shoot at you."

Track? These men had a lead on Kidd? Marsh wasn't sure how much credence to give that claim, but if it was true . . .

These men had just gained themselves a follower, like it or not.

"If you want to go after Henry Kidd, go after him," Marsh said. "I can't stop you. But you won't stop me, either."

"You stay away from us, and from Kidd," Rolph said firmly. "You don't, we'll make you regret it."

Marsh said no more. Simply stared at them.

"You understand us, ya?" York said.

Marsh just kept on staring.

The brothers looked at each other, laughed, and went on their way down the street, talking in a language Marsh could not understand.

He waited until they were nearly out of sight, and fell in behind them.

CHAPTER SIX

If they had a lead on Kidd, they didn't follow it right away. They wound their way to a saloon, drank for an hour, and came out staggering drunk. Marsh followed them again and smiled to himself as they entered the same hotel in which he had a room.

As drunk as they were, Marsh was sure they would not rise earlier than he, and he was right. By the time the sun had cleared the horizon, he was already up, out of his room, making a breakfast out of a cold biscuit he had filched from the cafe the day before. His horse was saddled, and he watched the hotel with infinite patience, nibbling his biscuit slowly.

They emerged about nine o'clock, a little earlier, actually, than Marsh would have guessed. Even from a distance their hangovers showed in the way they squinted, the way they moved, the grim looks on their faces. They went to the livery and emerged with their horses, took them back to the hotel, vanished inside, then came out again with a few goods packed in saddle-bags they threw over their mounts.

Booted Winchesters rode beside them on both saddles, and they wore large Colt revolvers in open defiance of the town's gun-carrying pro-hibition. But it didn't matter; this pair was ob-viously leaving town anyway.

They rode out, and Marsh followed, keeping at a distance and, he hoped, out of their sight for as long as possible. He had only a meager hope that they actually had some kind of lead on Henry Kidd's whereabouts, but a meager hope was better than none, which was all he had otherwise.

Marsh found it amusing that it took the sup-posedly crack manhunters more than two hours to realize they were being followed. Rolph, who had seemed the less dim of the pair, was the first to see him, and he twisted around in the saddle and pointed in agitated fashion. When York saw Marsh, he pointed as well. Two fools, Marsh thought. He could imagine their invisi-ble eyebrows knitting together as they tried to figure out what to do.

At first they did nothing. They simply rode on ahead, a little faster than before, as if they could outrun him that way. It was futile. Marsh stayed with them, actually a little closer than before because now there was no reason to hide. Eventually they did what he anticipated. Rolph took out his rifle, aimed it high, and fired it a good thirty feet over Marsh's head.

He didn't think they'd ever actually try to shoot him—they seemed like fools more than murderers—but he took the message and fell back. He let them get ahead, almost out of view, then fell in behind again, riding off the trail so that the meager brush hid him, at least part of the time.

He didn't know if they really knew where Henry Kidd was, but they did ride like men with a clear destination in mind. With nothing better to do, Marsh Perkins would continue to follow.

Port McGee had run the little blacksmith shop near his house for fifteen years, and he did good, steady business despite a crotchety attitude about life. All the citizens of the Black Fork community knew him and joked about him and his eternal sourness, made up for by his very sweet and friendly wife. Port knew his reputation and was smart enough to play along with it, acting sometimes more sour than he really was because, oddly, it was expected and good for business.

He had just immersed a horseshoe in a bucket of cold water when the young stranger came in, slipping off his hat and nodding in a friendly manner. Port nodded back, eyeing the remarkably ugly newcomer, who was clad in somewhat oversized clothing that had not been washed in weeks, and whose hair stuck out like stiff straw from his somewhat misshapen head.

The newcomer sniffed loudly and said, "Howdy, sir. I see you're making a horseshoe there."

"That's right."

"I need you to make one for me."

Port looked down at the young man's feet. "Don't make 'em in that shape."

This comment seemed to throw the young man. He frowned, mumbled something, then chuckled. The chuckle grew to a full laugh, but it wasn't pleasant to hear, as most laughs are, but a sporadic coughing sound, interspersed with loud sniffs. The newcomer swiped his sleeve under his nose, and Port noted with un-revealed disgust how crusted the sleeve was.

"You were joking me," the young man said. "Took me a minute to get it."

"Aw, I just don't smile enough when I tell my jokes," Port said. "Folks tell me that all the time. What happened? Your horse throw a shoe?"

"Yep."

"I'll take a look."

Port followed the young man outside. A pale mare stood there, looking underfed and ill-used. One shoe was gone. On its back, though, was a fine saddle, quite expensive and out of keeping with the ragged and impoverished look of both owner and horse.

Port took measurements, grunted, and rose. "I'll get your shoe made right now, if you don't care to wait."

"I'll wait," the man said. "Glad to have company. These are dangerous times hereabouts."

They went back into the smithy. "You're talking of Henry Kidd, I reckon."

"Yeah. Scares me to death to have such a killer roaming about. Makes me afraid to ride alone."

"I don't blame you. I keep an eye out myself."

"Hell, I'm as afraid of the posses and the lawmen as I am of the killer hisself," the visitor went on. "A man my age and size, out riding, why, they might think I was Kidd."

Port was hard at work on the shoe. "Could happen. I hear tell that over at Palmerville they shot a killer and didn't know until after that it wasn't Henry Kidd. They thought they'd killed the murdering son of a bitch." He glanced up at his visitor as he said this. "Too bad they didn't, huh?"

The fellow gave a flickering smile. "Yeah."

Silence held a few moments while Port hammered and shaped and worked the bellows and tongs. The visitor wandered over to the window that looked toward Port's house.

"What's that smell?"

"Dried apple pie," Port replied. "My wife makes it at least once a week. Best in Texas."

"I believe it. Smells real good."

There was a loud sizzle and hiss of steam as the horseshoe descended into the bucket. Port pulled it out again and laid it aside to cool.

The stranger turned and found Port standing there with a small revolver aimed at him.

"Hello, Mr. Henry Kidd," Port said. "I knowed it was you when you rode up."

"What the hell?"

"You heard me. Now get that gunbelt off, slow, and toss it over toward the corner. One hint of a slick move and I'll shoot this pistol and not quit until all six bullets are in you. You understand me, you murdering bastard?"

CHAPTER SEVEN

The visitor's face lost all color and his eyes went wide. He drew back his lips in a ghastly way, revealing his dirty and uneven teeth. And to Port's surprise, a great circle of dampness suddenly spread down his canvas trousers. The fellow had actually peed himself!

The first flicker of doubt came into Port's mind. Maybe this wasn't Henry Kidd after all. Would a cold-nerved killer who laughed at posses and vanished like a ghost time and time again pee his own pants just because somebody drew a pistol on him?

The newcomer fell to his knees. "Oh, God, oh, Lordy . . . don't kill me! I ain't no Henry Kidd! I swear it!"

"The gunbelt!"

Weeping now, face twisted and streaming

with tears, the terrified man fumbled at his buckle, loosened the gunbelt, and tossed it to the corner as he'd been instructed. Then he thrust his hands high in the air as if trying to touch the ceiling from his kneeling position. "Please," he said again and again. "Please don't kill me, don't kill me, don't kill me . . ."

"Shut up and stand," Port ordered, trying to sound authoritative and like a man with a definite plan, though in fact he was making this up as he went along. "Turn around and clasp your hands behind your back. Don't let go."

The young man nodded and complied. Port glanced about, looking for something to tie him with and also realizing he had a logistical problem: How could he tie up this man without laying down his pistol?

His wife was up in the house; they could go up there and he could have her hold the pistol while he tied up Kidd . . . if it really was Kidd. He certainly hoped it was. If not, he might have bought himself a whole wagonload of trouble he didn't need.

It all was very uncertain, though. Emily probably couldn't shoot anyone if she had to. But he wasn't willing to let her be the one to tie him, either. He didn't want her getting that close to him in case he grabbed at her.

He remembered something, all at once. Over in the shed was a pair of irons he'd made for a past sheriff. They'd gotten damaged along the way, had been brought in and repaired, then the sheriff lost the election and his replacement never came to collect the irons. They'd work perfectly to hold this man. Port would make him put them on himself.

"Out of here," he ordered. "Walk toward that shed."

"Oh, no, no . . . You're taking me out to shoot me!" The crying intensified.

"I ain't going to shoot you. I'm going to put you in irons and take you to the sheriff. He can sort this out. If you ain't Kidd, you can prove it to him, not me. I ain't taking no chances."

The fellow went a shade more pale. "I think I'm going to get sick."

"Don't do that. You've already got piss all over my floor. I don't want no vomit on it too."

"I'm feeling mighty weak."

Good Lord, the young man was actually about to faint! It was more doubtful by the moment that this was the infamous Kidd. Henry Kidd was cold and hard and shaken by nothing, or so folks said. This behavior didn't fit.

"Don't you pass out. Get up like a man."

"I'll try . . . I'll try . . ." He started to rise, then his eyes went out of focus, almost crossed. He moaned, and flopped over onto his belly. Right into the puddle of his own urine.

Port muttered a curse and went over to him, grabbing him by the back of the collar and yanking up. "Get up from there, you sorry son of—"

The young man rose swiftly, a lightning-flash move, and something bright in his hand flashed as well. Port grunted and staggered back, suddenly weak, and looked down to see profuse bleeding from his stomach.

The other was on his feet and at him in scarcely the time it took for Port to realize he'd been stabbed. The knife flashed again, again. Port dropped to the floor, limp as a rag, no longer able to hold the pistol. Yet he somehow managed to teeter on his knees and not fall over completely, not yet. His foe reached down and swept up the fallen pistol.

"I'd have left you alone if you'd left me alone," he said, a grin on his ugly face. "Hey, how'd you like the peeing? That throws them off every time. Ain't nobody believes that Henry Kidd would do that. But let me show you the kind of thing Henry Kidd does do!"

He glanced over and saw the hammer on the anvil. He picked it up, hefted it in his hand, and raised it. Meanwhile, he cocked the pistol and aimed it point-blank at Port.

He brought down the hammer hard on the anvil and pulled the trigger in tandem with the ringing blow, which masked the sound of the shot. Port fell over. The shooter laughed, proud of his timing, and tried it again. Once more, perfectly simultaneousness. The third time was just as well-timed.

"Did that well, didn't I!" he said to the dead man on the floor.

Then it struck him: The blacksmith was dead and the shoe was not on his horse. He'd have to do it himself as best he could.

Swearing violently, he fired another bullet

into his victim, along with another hammer ring, just for dying on him at an inconvenient time. Then, because it was his way to do such things, he kneeled and mutilated the face. Not as much as he sometimes did, for he felt potentially exposed here, with the wife in the house. Still, he made the blacksmith look horrific. At last he gathered up tools, nails, the horseshoe, and went outside. He moved his horse up a little so that it was hidden from view from the house, and did a clumsy job of putting on the horseshoe. He wasn't sure it would hold, and again cursed the blacksmith for having gotten himself killed a little too soon.

Briefly, the murderer returned to the smithy and poked around. To his delight he found an excellent Winchester rifle locked in a cabinet, with boxes of ammunition. He loaded up his new treasure, found a rifle boot that would fit his saddle in addition to the one he already had there, and returned to his horse outside.

He mounted, and glanced toward the house. The scent of that pie reached him again. He'd surely love a piece of it. But maybe there was somebody else in the house besides the wife. Instinct told him to forget the pie and go on. The wife was lucky; she'd live this time. Other times he might have just sent her soul over Jordan to join her husband's.

He rode back the way he'd come for a little over a quarter mile, then turned into a grove alongside a small stream.

"I got the shoe replaced," he said to the person awaiting him there.

"Good, Starky," the other replied. His way of speaking was that of a simpleminded man.

"We need to go on now. Get your horse. We need to ride. I got that feeling again. Somebody's after us and we need to move fast."

"There's blood on you, Starky. You smell like pee. You wet your pants, Starky."

"Never mind all that. Let's move."

"Did you hurt somebody again, Starky? Did you kill somebody?"

"Shut up! I'll not say it again: Let's move!"

CHAPTER EIGHT

Marsh had to hand it to the two Knutsen brothers. Dullards though they seemed, they'd managed to lose him, and that was no easy task when it came to Marsh Perkins, who folks back in Carolina claimed could track a will-o'-the-wisp through a windstorm. He was glad those same folks couldn't see him just now, outsmarted by two hard-drinking idiots with no visible eyebrows.

He stopped, made a fire by the roadside, and cooked some bacon. At the moment he was at a loss. No track of Henry Kidd, nor of the two men who claimed they had a notion of where Kidd was. Right now there was nothing to do but wait and keep his ears open for news of another Kidd murder.

It was a horrible way to track a man. Sometimes it made Marsh feel a little ill when he thought about it. Ill, and astonished, too. How could such a violent man have gone so long, so far, without being caught?

There was another mystery about Kidd: What had he done during the years between his wartime crimes back in Carolina, Tennessee, and—some claimed—Georgia, and the present, when he'd turned up murdering again in Texas? Had he lived peaceably during all that time, only to bloody his hands again all these years later?

Marsh nibbled his bacon and pondered it all. He doubted Kidd had gone a decade without killing. Murder seemed too much part and parcel with the man to imagine that he had ever gone long without it. No, Kidd must have been in some other part of the country, or maybe out of the country altogether. Mexico or someplace.

Marsh looked across the Texas landscape and felt very lonely. It was like that at these times, when the trail was cold. When he was on the chase, preoccupied with Kidd's next move, he thought little about home and all the miles he'd come. When the trail was cold, he had time to reflect, and to miss his kin and his beloved, familiar mountains. He couldn't wait to get back again. When he did, he'd never talk about this time of his life. He'd never bobble grandchildren on his knee and talk about the time he traveled all the way to the great West to find the murderer who had ravaged the home community. He knew others would tell the tale, and he couldn't do anything about that, but he'd not take part himself. He wanted only to finish this, then forget it.

With the meal done, he led his horse to a nearby stream and let it graze nearby while he leaned back against a tree, tilted down his hat, and took a brief, shallow nap.

He never lost full awareness of what was going on around him, but he did lose track of time. When he stirred back to awareness again, the sun had traveled far across the sky. The afternoon was well under way.

Marsh's horse was a trusty one and never wandered far. He mounted and rode, following nothing but instinct now. Kidd was to the west. He couldn't prove it, didn't really have any particular intuition about it, in fact. He just had to go somewhere. And the Knutsen brothers had headed west, so maybe that was the way to go. Couldn't hurt.

He wasn't sure what made him look behind him, but when he did, he saw a rider. Distant, hard to make out. For a moment he wondered if it could be Kidd, but when he squinted and looked hard he could see that the build wasn't right. This man was bigger than the wiry Kidd. He wore a long-tailed coat of some sort, perhaps a mackinaw or duster. Marsh watched him awhile, trying to ascertain if the man might be following him. He couldn't tell, but decided not to linger and let the man reach him. You never knew these days where you might find danger.

He'd gone a mile when a delicious scent

reached his nose. Cooking beef . . . maybe venison. The aroma of boiling vegetables and fresh biscuits mixed in, borne on wood smoke. He saw smoke clouds rising over the low hillside to the south. Lots of smoke . . . There was some sort of sizable gathering under way on the far side of that hill.

A glance ahead revealed a sign beside the road. He rode up close enough so that he could see it if he squinted. WOODHAWK, TEXAS, 2 MILES, the sign said.

He left the road and headed south, going up the rise to the top of the hill. There he stopped and looked down on a remarkable scene.

Wagons and tents were spread across a big expanse of land. Fires burned everywhere and people milled about, cooking, eating, talking. Quite a few were reading, and though he was still too far away to see clearly what they read, he knew right away it was the Bible. There was a big brush-covered platform standing in the midst of the gathering, with a pulpit in the middle and a big wooden cross standing at the rear, with a few chairs scattered along the rear of the stage.

A camp meeting!

Marsh hadn't encountered one of these extended religious gatherings since he'd run across one in Tennessee while on his way west. He smiled, feeling a certain nostalgic warmth for a familiar institution that reminded him of home.

In the absence of new leads on Henry Kidd,

he knew what he'd be doing the next couple of days. He'd visit this camp meeting, get to know some people, share some good food, and listen to a few stirring sermons. Who knew? Maybe he'd learn something here to help him find Henry Kidd.

He rode down toward the camp and was first noticed by a man who was dumping the dregs out of a coffee kettle. The man eyed him closely, with some suspicion, and Marsh knew just what he was thinking. Any lone young man in these parts these days could easily be suspected of being Henry Kidd. Especially a baby-faced one like Marsh. He was reminded anew of how careful he should be.

The man evidently decided that Marsh didn't look like a killer, for he smiled and nodded a greeting.

"Hello, brother, and good day to you," he said to Marsh.

"Howdy, sir." Marsh looked around. "Mighty big camp meeting."

"Yes indeed. Have you traveled here to join with us?"

"To tell you the truth, I wasn't even aware of it. I just sort of stumbled across it."

"It's a good one, now in its third day, and going strong." The man walked up to Marsh and put out his hand. "Bailey Jones. I live over at Woodhawk."

"Marsh Perkins, out of North Carolina."

"North Carolina! Well, I had some people

from there. Your speech is like theirs. What part of the state?"

"Western. The mountains."

"Beautiful place. But mighty remote and rugged. A lot different than Texas, huh?"

"Yes, sir."

The man had not, and would not, ask what had brought Marsh all the way from North Carolina. There was a code on the western plains that said a man's business was his own. Inquisitive people were not looked on in a kindly way. Even now, Marsh wasn't sure whether Jones was being truly friendly, or simply trying to get close enough to him to keep an eye on him in case he really wasn't who he said he was.

"I'd like to invite you to join the meeting," Jones said. "There's been much moving of the Lord's power here. People are turning to God in a time of distress."

"What distress would that be?" Marsh already knew, but he didn't want to be the one to bring up the matter of Henry Kidd.

"There's a terrible, pestilent murderer in these parts just now. People are afraid, and with cause. Have you ever heard the name Henry Kidd?"

"I have."

"Then perhaps you know what I'm speaking of."

"I was in Palmerville and heard the subject being discussed. There was a killing there, and people thought Henry Kidd had done it. But when the posse killed the murderer, it turned out to be someone else."

"I heard the same story myself, only this morning, from another family that rode in to join us. Kind of an ironic thing, I guess . . . Henry Kidd being so wicked is causing people to want to be more good. This camp meeting seems the place to be . . . for practical reasons as well as religious ones. There's safety in numbers. People feel safer in the midst of a crowd, safer than if they are isolated off in their own homes."

"Makes sense."

"Come join us. We've got food."

"I just had some bacon a while ago. Don't need anything right off."

"Join us anyway."

"I will."

"Maybe eat some supper with us later."

"I'll do that too."

CHAPTER NINE

Jones was one of those sincerely friendly people who have little pretense about them. If at first he checked Marsh over pretty thoroughly, at last he seemed to relax about him and take him at his word regarding who he said he was. Still no questions about purposes in being in the region and so on. And Marsh had not given up that information voluntarily.

If Bailey and his wife, a rotund woman named Virginia, were not prone to ask Marsh his business, their young daughter was not so reticent. She was about eleven years old, freckled and sandy-haired, and very forthright. The western code of silence wasn't a concept Martha Jones had yet fully grasped.

"What's your mother's name?" she asked Marsh at supper that night. The sky was darkening and singing was under way over near the pulpit area. Three preachers were warming up to deliver at top volume as soon as the music had everybody softened up for the message.

"Martha, don't ask questions like that," her mother said.

"It's all right," Marsh said. "I don't mind it. Her name is Emma June, Martha. Emma June Marsh. She was a Shelton before she married."

"I like the name Emma June. If I ever get a real doll, I might name her that."

"Honey, the dolls your papa makes you are real dolls," Virginia said.

"I mean a store-bought doll," she said. "With a china face."

She was a charming little thing. Marsh had a young cousin she reminded him of a lot. If he was near a store, and if the parents didn't mind it, he'd buy this girl a store-bought doll right now, with his own money. Of course, there was no store within miles except whatever typical kind of general store would be in Woodhawk, two miles down the way, and Marsh suspected it didn't sell dolls with china faces.

"What kind of work do you do?" Martha asked.

This time both parents chided her in unison. She looked puzzled and a little hurt.

But Marsh noticed both parents, then looked expectantly at him, unable to disguise their own interest in how he would answer.

"Well . . . right now I'm not really working, in the usual sense," he said, measuring every word. "I have some support from family and friends back home while I search for somebody."

"Oh," Martha said, not really understanding. "Is it your brother?"

"No."

"Your father or uncle?"

"Martha, that's enough," Virginia said.

"It's not a relative. Just somebody who was in our community one time," he said.

It was clear, he hoped, that he would say no more. He wasn't about to reveal the details of his mission, not in front of this child, and not in the setting of a camp meeting. He wasn't at all sure what kind of reaction he would receive.

"Martha, it ain't polite to ask people too much about their business," Bailey said. "Folks take offense to that."

"Ah, she's just asking questions like children do," Marsh said. He gave her a friendly wink. "No problem I can see."

Conversation moved to other subjects, but Marsh heard little of it. He'd just spotted someone a few campsites over who for the moment had his full attention.

Her hair was auburn, her skin somewhat pale and completely unblemished. Her gingham clothing was modest, as one would expect of a decent girl from a decent, camp-meeting-attending family, but it did not fully hide a beautiful, very feminine frame.

But it was her eyes that made his heart race a little faster. Big, perfect, heavily lashed eyes that for a few moments caught his, and held just long enough to make Marsh lose his breath.

He almost rose, almost went to her. But Marsh was shy; women at times actually scared him, though he had never dared admit it to anyone. Something in her eyes simply made him freeze, and when she turned and disappeared into the crowd, he was unable to pick her out again.

"Who was that?" he asked the Jones family in general.

"Who?"

"The young lady who was over there."

Bailey smiled. "Some young beauty has caught your eye, I take it."

Marsh was oddly embarrassed by the question. "Uh . . . no. No, she just looked like somebody I met before, and I wondered if it might be her."

Marsh had just lied in the midst of a camp meeting. He wondered how serious a sin it was.

"I don't see who you are talking about."

"She's gone now. Never mind. It wasn't important."

The preaching began, and Marsh learned just how deeply the presence of Henry Kidd had affected this part of Texas. The danger of the present moment was the subtle, or sometimes not-so-subtle, undertext of almost everything said, or shouted, from behind the pulpit. Marsh found himself caught up in the sermons, inspired by them, but not in the way most would be. His unique relationship to the subject at hand made the sermons quite personal to him, and when one of the preachers began openly talking about the "demon roaming these plains" and the "pale horse of death" that had the region in fear, Marsh trembled with awareness of the importance of his mission.

The third preacher, less fiery than the first two, preached a sermon not as obviously inspired by the depredations of Henry Kidd. Using the text "Here am I, send me," he sought to inspire evangelistic fervor among the flock.

But the preacher halted the sermon abruptly, saying he felt led to do something unplanned. He had the big outdoor congregation bow heads in prayer. "O Lord," he prayed, "send us a protector, an avenger. Send us hope in our time of fear. Send us one who will destroy the wicked man, Henry Kidd, who defies your law and murders the innocent, young and old. Send us one who will face him without fear, and persevere until the demon is slain. Send us one who will destroy the great evil, O Lord. Send us one who will go in the name of righteousness and avenge the innocent. Call his name, Lord, and let him answer."

Alone at the fringe of the crowd, Marsh Perkins bowed his head and quietly whispered, "Here am I, Lord. Send me."

Chapter Ten

Dawn, the next day. People across the camp-ground were beginning to stir, fires glowed, food sizzled on skillets. Marsh, always an early riser, had been up an hour already, as had the Jones family. Bailey Jones was talkative, but Marsh had an on-edge feeling he couldn't account for. There was something stirring in the air, a feeling not unlike that of a coming storm. But the sky was clear.

He saw her. An unexpected sighting, like the first one. She was walking across the camp, carrying a bucket of water dipped from the little spring that watered the campground.

In the dim light of morning she looked even more beautiful than she had the day before. She had not noticed Marsh just now, as best he could tell, so he stared rather openly at her, thinking how perfect a creation she was and how much he wished he had the courage to speak to her. A murderous, maiming devil like Henry Kidd he could trail with little fear, but a pretty girl made him tremble and lose his words.

He watched her until she reached her campsite, where a man, presumably her father, took the bucket from her. She immediately went to tend the breakfast that was frying in a big iron skillet over the fire. Her mother, herself an attractive woman, though somewhat plumped by the years, joined her daughter at the fireside. A boy of about ten, probably a little brother, was receiving instruction from his father about some task or another needing to be done, and not looking happy about it.

The sound of a horseman riding in fast finally drew Marsh's attention away from the lovely girl at the campfire. He turned to see a man coming in full speed, hardly slowing even as he entered the camp. He rode among the campsites at reckless speed and headed toward the arbor-covered pulpit, nearby which the preachers and leaders of this religious meeting had their tents.

That sense of foreboding that had affected Marsh increased. Something was afoot here, and the horseman's wild and desperate manner indicated it was not good.

Marsh quickly moved up through the camp in hope of getting near enough to hear what was being said. But by the time he did, the words had already passed.

The Rev. Jonah Cacey, a bearded, somber, barrel-chested man with a long gray beard and the manner of an Old Testament prophet, was mounting the stage. It was not time for preaching, but clearly he was about to say something.

"Attention!" he boomed from behind the pulpit. "All attention to me! Heed me, saints . . . I have news to give!" Cacey's voice was as loud as a cannon blast, emanating from that big, resonating chest of his. No wonder he had such success as a preacher. It was Cacey who had given the prayer for a divine protector the night before.

"Gather near, saints," he said. "Come close so that you can clearly hear what I tell you."

People moved in from their campsites, faces somber because it was evident from Cacey's look and tone that his news would not be good.

As focused on Cacey as he was, Marsh still managed to sneak a glance across the crowd until he spotted the lovely young lady. When he saw her looking back at him he quickly looked back to the stage. She did the same. Marsh's heart, already thumping fast, thumped a little faster yet.

Cacey's stentorian voice boomed. "There has been the work of Satan among the people of this region, yet again," he said sadly. "I must inform you of the murder and mutilation of Mr. Port McGee, the blacksmith many of you know well."

A gasp and murmur passed through the crowd, followed quickly by the sound of a few women beginning to cry, and children, tugging on their parents' coattails, asking in loud whispers for an explanation of what the preacher had just said.

"The evidence is that the work is that of the devil Henry Kidd, a man whose soul belongs to Beelzebub himself and who is the enemy of God and his people wherever he goes."

"God curse his soul!" a man shouted emotionally.

"My brother, the curse is already upon his soul, placed there not by God but by Henry Kidd himself, who has chosen the dark way over the light. And we bring a curse upon ourselves if we allow him to continue unmolested! The law has tried to find and destroy Henry Kidd; the law has failed. Hunters for bounty have gone after this human devil; they, too, have failed. Fathers now tremble in fear for their families, and children cry in their beds, comforted by mothers as fearful as they are. Can we allow this abomination to stand?"

"No!" many voices shouted in ragged unison.

"Then I call upon you, men of faith and courage, to go to your wagons. Fetch out your arms, put on the sword of faith, gird up your loins, and join me in pursuit of this demon from hell! We will form a mighty army of God, sweep this countryside, and sweep out this sinful creature! Let us ride out together and find this outlaw Henry Kidd!"

The roar that went up in response to this was deafening. Marsh was caught up in the same excitement that prompted it, but with it in his case was a strong sense of doubt. Though the preacher could call it an "Army of God" if he chose, in fact what he was proposing was just one more posse, and Henry Kidd had evaded posses time and again. It was one of his dark talents.

Still, a man never knew what might happen. Maybe this time it would be different. So Marsh, along with the rest, readied himself to ride, loaded up the revolver rifle, and sent up a prayer to heaven that today, at last, would be the day that Henry Kidd was brought down.

He was riding out with the big conglomeration of armed and determined men when he glanced to his left and noticed the object of his adoration watching him. Or was she looking at the group in general? No . . . she had her eye on him. He felt a thrill of excitement, and hoped that he looked sufficiently dashing to impress her.

The Army of God thundered away from the camp meeting grounds, Cacey leading the band with his long beard blowing in the wind.

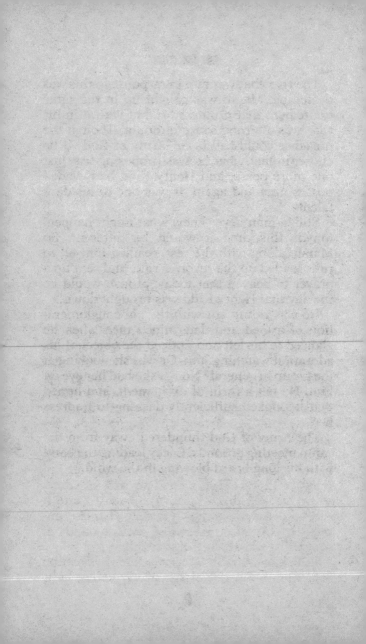

CHAPTER ELEVEN

Marsh was quite uncertain about this huge, informal, unofficial posse. No question that these men were motivated, and many of them were probably capable. The very size of the group, though, made it unwieldy and hard to hide. Henry Kidd would see this bunch coming from miles away. Marsh had his doubts that they would actually bring him in.

Nevertheless, there was something stirring about riding with such a purposeful and impressive group. Marsh felt like part of something big and fearful and righteous . . . and it did not take him long to realize that the immediate situation presented him a handy if somewhat self-serving opportunity.

Riding to Marsh's left and somewhat behind him was the father of the pretty young lady.

Here was a chance to introduce himself to the family, which might lead to meeting the girl a little later on.

Marsh drifted back, letting his horse fall in beside the man's. He looked for something to say, but before he could speak, the man spoke first.

"Quite a task we have before us, eh, young man?" he said to Marsh.

"Yes, sir." Marsh leaned over, hand thrust out. "Marshall Perkins, from North Carolina. Folks call me Marsh."

"Jim Serandon. You're a long way from home."

"Yes, sir. You live hereabouts?"

"Yep. Over the other side of Woodhawk. Got a little ranch."

"Family?"

"Wife and daughter. God knows it's a hard time to have a family, with a murderer roaming the countryside."

"I suppose your family is back at the campground."

"Yes. I'm grateful the meeting is going on. There's more safety with the crowd there. If not for that, I'd not be leaving them."

"You look like a young man—your daughter is small, I guess."

Serandon grinned widely. "Mr. Perkins, Marsh, you may as well come honest with me. I saw you taking notice of my daughter back at the campground. I figured she was the reason you drifted your horse over near me. Am I right?"

Marsh was stunned, and too taken aback to speak. There was no real shame in what he'd done, but it was still embarrassing to have the plain facts so openly laid out by none other than the father of the girl he admired.

"Well . . . I . . . the truth is . . . I'm sorry, sir. You're right. She's mighty beautiful, and I couldn't help but think she looked like a fine young woman. I beg your pardon, Mr. Serandon."

Marsh began to drift his horse back over, away from Serandon.

"Hold up, Marsh," Serandon said. "No need for that. I know she's a beautiful girl. She looks just like her mother did at her age, when first I laid eyes on her, and I was just as struck by her mother as you are. No need to go red-faced on me."

Marsh managed a grin, but couldn't think of a word to say. He rode along in silence, staring straight ahead, then started whistling softly in a forced nonchalance.

Serandon couldn't help but smile. "Marsh, maybe when this is done, you can join the family and me for supper."

"Maybe so. Kind of you, sir."

"I'll introduce you to Corinne."

Marsh nodded, no words. This was going well, in a way. Serandon was certainly open to him, and not averse to his interest in his daughter. He'd actually received an invitation to meet her. But it was all a little strange, and embarrassing.

It all faded into the background, though, when there was a flurry of loud voices and pointing fingers near the front of the band of riders.

Marsh at first could not ascertain what the commotion was about, but after moving a few paces spotted what those at the front had already seen: a lone man, mounted, out on the plains.

"It's Kidd!" someone declared. "We've found him, sure as the world!"

"Sweep down on him!" someone else hollered. "Don't let him outrun us!"

But the lone man on the horse didn't look interested in running. He sat slumped in the saddle, looking back at the Army of God, no doubt wondering what kind of strange conglomeration of armed humanity this was.

Marsh quickly rode forward, working his way through the band of riders until he reached the preacher Cacey. "Sir," he said. "My name is Marsh Perkins. I need to tell you that that man out there ain't Henry Kidd."

The preacher's gray eyes pierced him. "How do you know that, young man?"

"Because I've trailed Henry Kidd for months. I came from North Carolina, where he killed innocent folk back during the war, just to track him. I've not been real close to him, sir, but I've seen him from a distance and can tell you that ain't him. That man out there is far too big a fellow." Marsh looked at the distant figure and the distinctive long coat he wore. "I saw that man before, riding behind me, about the same distance he is from us now. I recognize his form and his coat. But I don't know who he is. But he ain't Kidd."

Others, who were not able to hear what Marsh said, just then whooped in unison and started to ride toward the man on the plains. Marsh looked at them in shock, afraid that some overeager avenger might actually gun the man down before asking any questions.

"Sir, you've got to stop them," he said.

Cacey, who had seemed uncertain the last few moments, suddenly became resolute. "Halt!" he called. "Desist, men! That isn't our man out there!"

The riders stopped, turning and looking bewildered. "That could be him!" one said.

"No," Marsh said. "I've seen Henry Kidd. That ain't him."

"Then who is he?"

"I don't know."

"I suggest we go find out," the preacher said. "But slowly, and without threat. If he isn't Kidd himself, perhaps he will have seen something of him. Don't frighten him, men. Keep your guns ready, but not leveled." Marsh swung out and joined the small band of riders, led by the preacher, who slowly traveled toward the lone man.

CHAPTER TWELVE

If the stranger was concerned by the approach of armed strangers, he didn't show it. His posture in the saddle was utterly relaxed; he exuded a confidence and fearlessness that Marsh could detect from far away, and had to admire.

It was obvious before long that this man was a Mexican, though perhaps not fully. His eyes and nose had a distinctly Anglo quality about them.

He was a fine-looking fellow, dark haired and somewhat swarthy. His clothing was dirty from the trail, yet fit his broad-shouldered, narrow-waisted form quite finely. He smiled at the riders who approached him.

The preacher spoke first. "Hello, sir. My name is the Reverend Jonah Cacey, servant of the Lord. These men here with me are saints and citizens of these parts, and we ride together in search of one Henry Kidd, an outlaw and murderer."

The man lifted one dark brow. "You say much in a few words, Reverend. I am impressed." His English, though lightly accented with the intonations of Mexico, was elegantly spoken. He put out a strong hand toward the preacher. "I am Juan Carlos, and am honored to make your acquaintance, sir."

The preacher shook Carlos's hand. "We held suspicion about you, sir, when we saw you from a distance, that you were in fact Henry Kidd."

"Any lone traveler in these parts is subject to that suspicion . . . which is a danger, eh, sir? Fear and caution can cause danger to the innocent . . . yet Kidd seems to roam free with impunity."

"You are aware of his depredations, I take it."

"Very aware, sir."

"Do you know anything of his possible immediate whereabouts? Seen or heard anything?"

"I know nothing. Only that Henry Kidd is a man pursued by determined avengers." As he said this, he looked directly at Marsh, which surprised Marsh, who wondered if the look was coincidental or meaningful. Coincidental, surely. How could this man know anything of who he was, or his quest?

"There has been another murder," the preacher told Carlos. "A local blacksmith has been killed and his body left damaged, as is Kidd's wicked way."

"You are a posse, then? I ask your pardon for this question, sir, but why would a posse be led by a priest?"

"Not a priest," Cacey said, somewhat snappily. "I am no Papist, sir. I am a preacher of the word of God. The men you see here are good men of this region who were already gathered for worship at an extended camp meeting a short distance from here. When we learned of the latest murder, we felt it our obligation to respond as a divine army, sweeping to find and stop Henry Kidd once and for all."

"My best wishes for your success," Carlos said. And he glanced at Marsh again.

There was something beneath the surface here. Marsh could tell it. Juan Carlos, whoever he was, seemed to know him, or at least know what he was doing. Marsh wondered who Carlos was and why he was here, riding alone at a place and time in which riding alone could get a man killed by an overly nervous populace.

"You are welcome to join us," Cacey told Carlos. "All help is welcome, and you are safer with a large band such as ours."

"Thank you, sir. But I have business that requires me to remain as I am."

As the smaller delegation of riders rejoined the larger body awaiting them, Marsh looked back. Juan Carlos was riding slowly away, circling toward the southwest, moving slowly. Marsh frowned, overwhelmed with curiosity about the man, wondering if he would encounter him again.

Cacey led his "army" onward, a band of Christian soldiers sweeping the plains with a sense of pride and cockiness that faded somewhat when finally they rode into view of the blacksmith shop where Port McGee had died.

The county sheriff was talking gently to the weeping widow when the Army of God came up like a band of angry angels. The corpse had just been removed by the local undertaker and was on its way to town in the back of an enclosed black wagon. The sheriff, who had been seated beside the widow on a rickety bench outside the smithy, came to his feet as the big band of riders rumbled in.

His face went red and his eyes wide. The Reverend Cacey rode right up to the sheriff and dismounted with great dignity, and the sheriff all but grabbed his collar.

"Preacher, pardon my French, but what the hell do you think you're doing?"

Cacey puffed up and seemed to gain about a foot of stature. "We, sir, have come to learn the grim facts of this case, and to chase down and destroy the outlaw Henry Kidd." He paused and looked at the widow. "My condolences, ma'am, in this horrible time of loss. God will sustain you, if you let him."

Another man, wearing the badge of a deputy, emerged from the smithy. He gaped to see the Army of God. "The tracks!" he bellowed. "Sheriff, they just trampled over all the tracks!"

"So they did," the sheriff replied. To Cacey he said, "Do you see that, Preacher? We had a good, clear set of tracks left by the murderer, and now they're gone. All your horses here have trampled them away."

Cacey looked bewildered, but only for a moment. He wasn't one to let himself look disadvantaged in front of his audience.

"Well . . . regrettable, then. But it doesn't matter. With a band this large we can sweep this countryside and find this devil, with or without tracks."

"Preacher, that devil has evaded posse after posse. You might catch him, you might not. Suffice it to say that without tracks, the likelihood is strongly lessened."

"Regrettable," the preacher said again. "Regrettable." He cleared his throat and looked vainly for something else to say.

"Regrettable, you say. Yes, indeed. If we fail to catch this bastard, Preacher, because of you trampling up his trail, I'll hold you personally responsible."

The preacher looked a little pale, but soon collected himself. "Perhaps you should quit your profane complaining about our arrival and make use of us, Sheriff. I have an army of men here willing to look for the devil Henry Kidd until he is found. If we've trampled a few tracks, what of it? You saw which way they went, did you not? Let this army of righteous men sweep the entire countryside. We'll uncover him. We'll sweep the evil being straight into perdition."

"You may not have noticed just how big this entire countryside is, Preacher," the sheriff responded. "Your group is big, but the countryside is a hell of a . . . pardon me, a way whole lot bigger. Henry Kidd will see you coming long before you see him, and he'll vanish, like he always does."

"I have every confidence God will deliver him into our hands."

"Beg pardon, Preacher, but I'd have been glad for the Lord to deliver him into my hands at any time, and so far he ain't seen fit to do it."

The preacher and the sheriff argued, growing more vigorous by the moment. The widow wept, the deputy stood around looking angry . . . and Marsh moved toward the rear perimeter of the group of horseman, staring off toward hills limned against the sky.

He'd just seen something.

CHAPTER THIRTEEN

The glint of light on glass is what had drawn Marsh's attention. To the west was a line of low but rough-and-rocky hills, well covered with brush. From a gap between two rocks he'd caught that quick flash of reflected sunlight, and a closer look revealed two familiar forms, kneeling in the brush and watching the commotion around the smithy.

He wondered if the Knutsen brothers had noticed him in particular, and if they'd had any luck in finding Kidd. Probably not. If they had Kidd, they'd be trumpeting it proudly, hauling in his corpse over the back of a horse and heading for the nearest saloon for some liquid celebration.

Marsh kept watch on the poorly hidden brothers, while also listening to the argument between the sheriff and the preacher. It seemed the preacher was on the losing end, the sheriff telling him that he had no use for posses formed outside the bounds of the law. Cacey's answer was that he served a higher law, but that did little to persuade the sheriff. It seemed likely to Marsh that the Army of God had gone as far as it would go.

Good enough for him. He didn't believe they would catch Kidd anyway. Time to discharge himself from the army and begin following the brothers again. Maybe they had a lead to Kidd, or would stumble across one.

Quietly, Marsh rode away from the group, trying to draw no attention. It wasn't easy, and he was also aware that there was no way to do this without the Knutsen brothers seeing him. Probably they'd vanish well before he got near them, but at least he might be able to track them.

"Marsh!"

The voice came from the perimeter of the crowd. Marsh turned in the saddle. It was Serandon, riding out after him.

"Where you going?"

Marsh was irritated. He'd hoped he could just disappear. He saw no alternative but to tell the truth.

"There are a couple of brothers I met who are looking for Henry Kidd, like we are. They told me they had a lead on his whereabouts. Well, they're watching us right now, through field glasses, over in those hills."

Serandon looked in the direction Marsh subtly indicated. "I don't see . . . wait. Yes, I do. I see them!"

"I'm going to try to work around where I can follow them."

"You think they really know where Kidd is?"

"No. If they did, I doubt they'd be lying in brush watching us. But they've got a better chance of finding him than this big group does."

Serandon looked intrigued. He glanced back at the arguing sheriff and preacher. The fire was certainly being diminished in the Army of God. He turned back to Marsh.

"I'll go with you."

"Sir, there's no need for it. I've tracked Henry Kidd alone all this time, and I don't know I'd work well with somebody else."

"You've tracked Kidd? What do you mean?"

"I've been tracking Henry Kidd for months now. I came here from North Carolina to do it."

"Why?"

"He killed my father and some other good people back where I come from, a long time ago. I was sent to find him and avenge the dead."

Serandon rode out close to Marsh. "You telling me the truth?"

"Yes, sir."

"I'll be! Now I really do want to go with you. That's impressive, son! You're on a righteous quest . . . it's downright biblical!"

"I need to go, sir. I hope to see you again, and

maybe take you up on your offer of hospitality with your family."

"I'm coming with you."

"Sir, I—"

"No arguing. It's safer with two. I'm coming with you."

Marsh sighed. Clearly there was no point in arguing. And probably it didn't matter. The Knutsen brothers probably had no more idea than did Cacey or the sheriff where Henry Kidd really was. He and Serandon would poke around a bit, follow the Knutsens if it was feasible, then head back to the campsite. "Very well, sir. But let's be as quiet as we can about it."

"Wait just a minute." Serandon went to another man and spoke to him. Marsh could make out enough of what was said to determine that Serandon was sending a message back to his family, not to worry about him if he did not return as soon as the entire band.

Serandon joined Marsh, his manner eager. Marsh had the odd sense that he, by far the younger of the pair, had a much more mature perspective on what was going on here. Serandon seemed to view it as something of a lark.

They rode out together, slipping southward until the swell of the land hid them, then circling back toward the hills where the Knutsens hid.

They reached the hills and found tracks there, but the two manhunter brothers were not in sight.

"We'll follow as far as we can," Marsh said. "If we find them, maybe we'll find Kidd, too. They claimed to have a lead on him, but I've got my doubts."

"Why would they say it, then?"

"Reward. They want it for themselves. I think they were trying to put me off to lessen the competition. They were afraid I'd get him before they did. And they're right. I will be the one who gets him. My granny dreamed it, and her dreams always happen."

"I'll be. She's never wrong?"

"Not so far."

They rode out, following the trail, but as all Marsh's trails had lately, it grew cold. Hours passed, the day rolling by. Marsh had food in his saddlebags, not much of it, and when shared with Serandon it went twice as fast. He wished the man would just go away.

He had a bad feeling about him being here. It was something that just wasn't supposed to be.

While the sun declined toward the western horizon, the newspaper had literally blown into the hidden little camp that hid the two Kidd brothers. It had so startled Starky Kidd, the venomous young man known to the world as Henry, that he had whipped around and drawn a pistol when it came blowing into the brush, hanging up and flapping there. He quickly collected the newspaper, most of which was gone, and looked at the date. It was only a week old, part of a weekly printed in the next county. Starky Kidd, who could read a little, with effort, sat down and spread the paper before him, grinning as he took in the headline he'd hoped he'd find.

"Listen at this!" he said. "It says, 'Henry Kidd, Murderer of Six or More Men, Has Region . . .'" He paused, squinting and mouthing out letter sounds. ". . . 'Has Region Quaking in Terror.'"

Starky's brother looked puzzled. "What does that mean?"

"It means we got everybody around here scared bad, Henry. It means folks are looking for Henry Kidd because he kills people."

"I don't kill people."

"Why, it says right here that you do! Right here in the newspaper! Says you killed at least six men! Now, why did you go and do such a thing, Henry?"

"I didn't! I ain't killed nobody! It's you, Starky! You're the one who hurts people and does bad things! I don't like the things you do!"

"I do what I got to do, Henry. Can't help myself. Never could!"

"So why does the paper say it's me?"

There was an easy answer to that question, but Starky Kidd, murderer, wouldn't give it. Simpleminded though his brother was, it might just be possible that he would understand the answer, and that was something Starky did not want ever to happen.

"Why, it must be a mistake! Now everybody thinks it's you, Henry! Everybody who reads this paper believes it's Henry Kidd who done all them bad things. Know what they'll do if they catch you, Henry?"

"No."

"They'll hang you! They'll say, 'There's Henry Kidd, the murderer . . . let's hang him!' And they will."

Henry's eyes were wide and full of fear. "Starky, you got to tell them it ain't me! You got to tell them I never killed nobody!"

"It's too late, Henry. Nobody would believe it. So I reckon you're stuck in the mudhole, huh? Now all you can do is to mind your brother. You do what I say, always and every time, and I can keep you safe. If you don't . . . well, there's a lot of ropes out there, and a lot of tree limbs."

Henry Kidd was pale and breathing hard. "Don't let them hang me, Starky. Promise me you won't let them hang me!"

Starky Kidd smiled darkly. "Why, I wouldn't let them do that, Henry. I'm your brother! I've took care of you since we was both boys! Have I ever let anybody hurt you?"

"No."

"Then you don't worry. You just always do what I say, and you'll be all right."

"I will, Starky. Don't let them hang me."

"I won't . . . if you'll always mind me."

CHAPTER FOURTEEN

Henry sat back against a tree, his knees pulled up close to his chin in the posture he always took whenever he was scared. Starky read the newspaper laboriously, enjoying learning of the terror he was spreading across this part of Texas. At last he laid the newspaper aside and looked over at Henry, who had fallen asleep.

He pondered his younger, simple-minded brother, feeling the combination of love and loathing he always felt toward him. The love came from the fact that they were brothers, had endured together the horrors of life under the beating rod of a drunken father, and had fled together on the stormy night that he had used the ax from the woodpile to finally end their father's existence. An eventful night, that one had been. Starky's first killing. And later, as he and his brother fled through a stormy Kentucky forest, a lightning bolt had stolen young Henry's intelligence in one swift stroke, leaving him alive but forever a child.

Starky had cared for his brother ever since that night, and it amazed him, when he thought enough about it, that they were still alive and together after all these years. Together they had left Kentucky, settled in Tennessee. There Starky had committed his second murder, a woman killed in a rage when she refused to give him the intimate favors he desired because he was "just a slip of a boy." His stabbing knife had by accident mutilated her face as she collapsed, and he'd found that intriguing. From then on, mutilation had been part of the ritual of almost all the murders he committed.

It was in North Carolina that he'd struck upon the strategy of taking on his brother's name when he killed. Just a little safety measure, that's all it was. Henry Kidd was a burden to him, after all, so why not get some use out of him? Let his name be the one associated with the murders . . . and maybe, if ever things went truly bad, it would be Henry's neck, and not Starky's, that would feel the pinch of the noose. Starky didn't want that to happen . . . but if ever it did, better his brother than himself. Brotherly love went only so far, after all. And at times, when Henry was his most whining and fearful and cloying, Starky didn't feel he loved his brother at all. Three times in the last six months he had stared at him while he slept and thought about trouncing him unconscious, stringing him up from a limb, and leaving a note from "Henry Kidd," announcing his suicide. Starky would be free then. Everyone would think the great murderer was dead, and he could go his way free of worry.

He might just do it yet.

Thunder rumbled suddenly, far away. Starky looked with concern toward the darkening western horizon, then at the sleeping Henry. He hoped the storm would pass. Lightning terrified Henry beyond anything else. If a big storm rose, Henry would become overwhelmed with fear, hard to console, hard to control. Starky didn't want that right now.

He watched the clouds, hoping the storm would blow on by.

The storm did not blow by. As darkness descended, the winds rose higher, buffeting the landscape and all those who ranged upon it. Night was coming, and it would be a wet and windy one, with plenty of lightning.

Marsh held his hat on with his left hand and stared out across the wide plains from the vantage point of the hills.

The Army of God was long gone. Marsh and Serandon had watched its departure less than an hour after they'd slipped away from the group that morning. Obviously the sheriff had managed to overwhelm Cacey's authority, or passion, or both. . . . In any case, the riders had moved in a great mass back toward the site of the camp meeting.

"Maybe you should go back to the campsite," Marsh had suggested to Serandon. "This storm could cause a real mess, if it turns out as bad as it appears."

Serandon shook his head. "There's plenty of people there, and they'll help each other. I'm a lot more concerned about getting rid of this murderer than I am the storm. I'll stay with you."

"Well, I appreciate that, but—"

"Look!" Serandon said suddenly, pointing south. "He's still out there."

Marsh saw him: Juan Carlos, still alone, riding in his perpetually relaxed manner across the plains, the dramatic and darkening sky spreading above him, the massive landscape around him. He was heading in Marsh's and Serandon's direction.

"I wonder who that man really is?" Marsh said. "There's something about him that just makes questions start coming to mind."

"There are some caves in these hills," Serandon said, looking at the sky. "Some of them big enough to hold men and horses, too. Unless we want to get wet, I suggest we find one of them. If you'll follow me, I think I know where one is."

Just then a huge lightning flash seared through the sky and struck a tree about a mile away. The flash and electric tingle in the air made Marsh's hair stand on end.

"Lead on," he said to Serandon as he tried to calm his spooked horse.

The pair rode back farther into the hills, Serandon leading the way.

CHAPTER FIFTEEN

It was times like these when Starky Kidd hated his brother.

Henry was terrified, inconsolable, screaming with every flash of lightning. His fear of lightning was primal, unerasable, branded into him years before by the hot stab of heat and electricity that had damaged his brain. Even in minor storms his suffering was great; in large ones such as this he was like a tortured soul on the brink of hell.

He was also a danger to his brother at these times. Starky Kidd lived a life in the shadows, a life of hiding, and a man couldn't hide very well with a screaming babbler at his side. Starky's rage was rising, and he played with the thought of taking out his pistol and ending Henry's screaming forever. He could dump the corpse out on the plains where it could be found, and folks would believe the killer plaguing the region had been shot by some helpful soul, for Starky and Henry bore a strong resemblance to each other. Starky would be able to relax a little . . . at least until he murdered again.

But even in the dark soul of Starky Kidd there was a flicker of primitive morality, at least where his brother was concerned. His brother was the only other living human being who had endured with him the sufferings of their childhood. No one else had been at his side all these years. As substandard a piece of human company as Henry was, he was at least a companion, someone who kept Starky from being utterly alone in the world. And so Henry let him live on, as he would let him live on tonight—unless he grew so out of control that Starky had no choice but to quieten him the only way possible.

The storm had driven the Kidds from their original hidden campsite. The same factors that had made it hidden also made it prone to flash flooding, and that had come shortly after the first torrents began to fall. The Kidd brothers had scrambled out of their little hollow, drenched to the skin. Starky saddled their horses in the rain, and off they went, looking for new shelter in the darkness, fearing the lightning—Henry screaming like a scared child all the while—and Starky hoping there were no hidden eyes in the low, brushy hills to see the region's most wanted outlaw scrambling across the plains by the light of the storm.

A lightning bolt flashed, moving horizontally across the sky. Henry screamed, bending forward on his horse, covering the back of his head with his hands. "Don't let it hit me!" he screamed. "Starky! Don't let it hit me!"

"Shut up, you damned fool!" Starky called. "Keep riding. Look yonder—I seen a cave over there when the lightning flashed. We'll go there."

But just then, he saw something else in the darkness, a dim, flickering square of light farther ahead.

"I'll be damned . . . there's a ranch house yonder," he said. "Maybe some food for us out in a shed or smokehouse or something. I'll take you to the cave, Henry, and then I'll go to the house and see what I can find." The talk of looking in sheds and smokehouses was for Henry's benefit. Starky had no qualms about looking in the house itself, and simply killing any occupant who got in the way of it.

"Don't leave me alone!" Henry wailed.

"Shut up and head for that cave."

"I don't see it!"

"Follow me. I'll get you there."

The cave was easily reached and surprisingly dry, thanks to the angle of the cave floor. With effort they were able to get their horses beneath a rocky overhang and at least mostly out of the bad weather.

Henry, though, was not much better off than

before. From inside, the cavern entrance formed a wonderful frame for the wild activity of the storm outside. Henry stared wide-eyed and blubbering at the lightning and rain, tears mixed with the rainwater on his face, his lower lip bulging out like that of a cowardly boy. Starky looked at him in disgust, and barely restrained himself from hitting him.

"I'm going to that spread now, and I'll bring us back some food," he said.

"Don't go, Starky!"

"I'm going. You sit down yonder and close your eyes. Don't watch the storm. You'll be fine, and the storm will pass."

Starky headed out of the cavern and into the rain.

Henry sank to the cave floor and buried his face in his hands.

A quarter mile away, Marsh Perkins and Serandon huddled in a cave quite similar to that occupied by Henry Kidd, but more spacious. Their horses were safely back deeper in the cavern, and except for a rivulet of water that ran back in from the mouth of the cave, the temporary partners were dry and relatively cozy.

But Marsh was very frustrated. He was convinced that he could have successfully gotten back on the trail of the Knutsen brothers if only he'd been alone. Serandon, though a well-intentioned and good-hearted man, was not a manhunter. He was loud and visible and clumsy and in the way. Now Marsh was stuck in a cave, waiting out a storm, with no idea of what he'd do or where he'd go when the storm ended. Another cold trail . . . not to mention wet. Come morning, he had no notion as to how he'd continue his quest. One thing was sure: He'd find a way to dump off Serandon.

"Wonder how it's going back at the camp meeting," Serandon said.

"Most likely they're getting a little wet. But I'm sure they're fine."

"The lightning worries me. It's dangerous to be out there on the flats when there's lightning."

"Yes, sir. But I feel sure they'll come through fine."

"I'll head back come morning. . . . I'd like to keep on helping you hunt, but I need to check on my family. You'll come too, maybe? Meet the family, eat a meal or two with us?"

Marsh thought about it. Why not? The storm was washing away much hope of successful manhunting. Back at the camp there would be food and companionship—and that promised chance to meet Corinne Serandon. "I'll come too. Thank you."

"Things haven't quite gone the way the preacher thought, have they? The 'army' didn't ever make it to battle."

"It's likely to be one man, or two, who bring down Henry Kidd," Marsh said. "He's too sly to be caught by a big, loud, visible group."

The rain continued, even intensified. The lightning was strong, and closer, the air very damp and cold. Marsh huddled under his coat, waiting for the storm to end and wondering where the mysterious Juan Carlos was. He smiled slightly to himself, picturing him riding with that same utterly relaxed posture through the midst of a driving storm. Every time he'd seen Carlos, that's the way he'd been.

He wondered who Carlos really was. He had a feeling about that man, and recalled how Carlos had looked meaningfully at him. Maybe their paths would cross again, and if so, Marsh might have a few questions for the mysterious Anglo-Mexican.

CHAPTER SIXTEEN

Starky Kidd was halfway to the ranch house when the lightning flared with particular brightness and revealed the unexpected sight of two men standing beside two horses, pressed up against the side of a small bluff in a vain attempt to escape the brunt of the rain.

The lightning flared for several seconds, giving him a good look at the pair, and them in turn a good look at him.

It might have amounted to nothing, this chance meeting with two strangers, but in the world of Starky Kidd, chance meetings seldom amounted to nothing. And such was the case now, for as soon as the pair spotted him, one of them shouted out spontaneously, "It's Kidd!" And he knew then that they were among the many who looked for him.

The man's shout had a funny sound to it, some kind of foreign-sounding inflection.

He reacted quickly, veering to the side and running through the darkness toward the nearest rocky hill. He ran blind, based on his memory of the terrain as revealed by that last lightning flash, and avoided running straight into a stone mass only when another lightning bolt fired down its light just in time to let him see the stone before him. He cut to the side and worked his way up and around the stone, seeking a hiding place. A glance back, another flash of lightning, and he saw that they were coming after him, on foot, with rifles in hand and horses abandoned back at the base of that bluff.

If the scenario were only slightly different, he might be able to circle around unseen and reach those horses, steal one and send the other running away. He couldn't do it, though—not easily, anyway—because the two pursuers were between him and the horses.

The best bet was to find a hiding place and let the storm and darkness serve as his protectors. If he got the chance, he'd kill one or both of these men, but under the circumstances he doubted it was wise to shoot unless he had a truly good opportunity. Shooting would reveal his location, and the odds of drawing a bead on, and then shooting, his targets in the brief span of a lightning flash didn't strike him as good.

He was clambering blindly around a boulder, seeking a hiding place, when the first shot was fired. One of the two men fired in tandem with a lightning flash, and very nearly hit him. He heard the bullet ricochet off stone not a foot from his head, and felt the sting of splintered rock against his face.

Starky swore, flipped the leather hold-down strap off his pistol, pulled it out, and fired randomly in the direction from which the shot had come. It was an act of anger, not planning, and as soon as he did it two more shots fired back at him, aims guided by the flash of his own pistol. One of the shots struck even closer than the first one.

He dove behind a rock, abrading himself, pinching his foot in a space between two boulders, and slamming his shoulder hard against a rock. It was hard to maneuver in the darkness—but he reminded himself that the same things that disadvantaged him also disadvantaged the two manhunters after him. He'd been in tighter spots—and at least Henry wasn't here to be in the way.

Starky's heart pumped, energy coursing through him. He was frightened, fully aware of the danger he was in, but he was also full of a strange, cold energy that usually overtook him at such times. It sometimes literally felt like a cold hand gripping the back of his neck, filling him with an icy courage and aggression that actually made him enjoy the danger. At such times he would grow bold and reckless, but in that very transformation become a more fearsome warrior. That energy carried him through, filled him with a dark joy and satisfaction that found its apex in the acts of murder and mutilation.

Two against one. That was the worst of this situation. One could engage him in a firefight, making him expose his position, while the other slipped around and gunned him down.

He had to change those odds. He had to play this his way, not the way they wanted him to. They were counting on him to panic, to shoot at them wildly as he already had, and thus to reveal his position very precisely. That, then, was the very thing he would not do.

Another shot fired, singing overhead. Starky Kidd grinned to himself there in the darkness. Let them shoot. He would be patient.

The odds would shift in his favor very soon.

At the sound of the first shot, Marsh came to his feet. "That ain't no thunderclap," he said.

"No, sir. That's a shot."

The follow-up shots confirmed what Marsh had already suspected. "No hunter is out in the midst of a rainstorm. And that pattern of shooting . . ."

"A gunfight," Serandon said.

"That's right."

"Kidd."

"Very likely."

"So what do we do?"

Marsh did not have time to answer. He was already heading out of the cavern into the rain, his hand wrapped around the cylinder of his unusual rifle to keep it as dry as he could.

Serandon stood there uncertain, and suddenly—if he dared admit it to himself—very afraid. A gun battle! And this time there was no massive "Army of God" surrounding him. Just him, Marsh Perkins, the darkness . . . and whoever was shooting.

He trembled so badly he could hardly move, and his breath came hard. He knew what he should do, but he couldn't find the courage to move. He stared out into the darkness, praying for strength to do his duty . . . but still not moving.

Huddled in his own cavern, cringing from the storm and lightning, Henry Kidd also heard the shots. He sucked in his breath and said in a sharp whisper, "Starky! Starky!"

Despite the storm, he came to his feet and edged toward the mouth of the cave. Starky was out there, and there was shooting. . . . He had to help his brother.

How, though? What could he do? And the lightning was so terrifying. . . .

But Henry Kidd was nothing if not loyal to the brother who took care of him. Despite the storm, he would have to move. He had to find a way to help Starky.

Though he had never been taught to pray, Henry Kidd did pray as best he could, an unconscious pleading for safety and for his brother. Armed by it, he bit his lip, whimpered softly, and plunged out into the violent, rain-driven night.

CHAPTER SEVENTEEN

Starky Kidd was not moving, scarcely breathing. His heart, though, hammered like a drum played too fast. The position in which he lay had him mostly on his back, looking upward, rain hammering into his face and eyes, making him blink to keep his vision as clear as possible. But he didn't need to see much to do what he had planned.

He gnawed his lip, hand gripping the pistol tightly, the other cupped over the end of the barrel to keep rain out of it. There he waited, ready, and listened to the slow approach of a man who would soon be dead.

Rolph Knutsen crept slowly through the rocks at the base of the hill, heart in his throat and his pulse racing like a scared Texas jackrabbit. He

was more scared than he would ever admit . . .
but excited as well. They'd done it! In the most
unlikely way, they had actually stumbled across
the murderer they had chased for months. He
was trapped, and they were closing in. Rolph
was already spending the reward money in his
mind, and talking big, braggadocious talk to the
pretty saloon girls who would be so impressed
by the man who killed Henry Kidd.

He could not see York now, not even when
the lightning flashed. The terrain was too rocky
and rough, and blocked his view. But he knew
where Kidd was, and in a moment he would be
in position to make his move. A quick lunge, a
fusillade into Kidd's cramped hiding place, and
it would be done. The morning sun would find
him and York bearing the corpse of the west's
most vile killer in for reward.

He reached the spot. Lightning flashed, so
close it startled him. He swallowed hard, said a
fast and fervent prayer . . .

Time to move.

With a great heave, he lunged forward.

Marsh heard the shots, three of them in quick
succession. He caught a glimpse of the flash of
the shots as well.

A lightning flare made him aware of someone
behind him. He turned quickly, in time to see
the outlined figure of Serandon, clambering
down through the rocks toward him.

He almost swore, his grandmother's firm

teaching on that subject notwithstanding. He'd wanted Serandon to stay put. This was not his kind of affair, and he would only be in the way. But he didn't want to shout to him and betray his presence to the others.

Maybe the shots would drive Serandon back into his hiding place. Marsh wondered who had fired them, and at whom.

"Rolph!" he heard a voice shout. It was York Knutsen. "Rolph, did you get him?"

There was no reply.

"Rolph?" York called again, and Marsh thought him a stupid man, for every shout revealed his general location. If Kidd had killed Rolph—and who else could it be but Kidd?—York was all but waving a target above his own heart and daring him to put a slug through it.

Marsh moved forward, forgetting about Serandon, hoping to get himself into a strategic position without being detected.

Henry Kidd, the real one, wanted to scream but could not. He was too scared, his throat too tightly constricted. He did not know if his brother was alive or dead, or if whoever was here—he had a feeling of men being all around him—would want to hang him like Starky had said they would.

Then came lightning, the biggest and closest blast of it so far. It struck a tree atop a nearby knoll and exploded it in a flash of fire. In the brilliant, blinding light, Henry made out the spectacular but horrifying sight of the knoll itself splitting apart under the impact of the bolt.

It was just like the bolt that had struck him when he was young, and it sent a primal terror through him that took away any rationality or self-control he possessed.

He began to run, blindly and without thought, heading by instinct toward the dim, yellow light of the ranch house to which Starky had said he would go. He ran as hard as he could, saying not a word nor giving any outcry. He ran long and hard, leaving the hills behind and making the yellow square of windowpane light before him grow ever larger.

Something huge and dark loomed up beside him. He had reached a barn. Another lightning flash sent him scurrying inside it. He scrambled into an empty stall and cast himself down in the straw, burying his face in it and wailing almost like an infant.

Her name was Marian Stevenson, and she had lived in the ranch house with her husband, Ned, for a decade. At the beginning Ned had done most of the ranching, leaving her to the domestic chores, but time had brought illness to her husband, and now he lay perpetually in his bed, on his back, looking at the ceiling and not speaking, usually not even looking around.

He was a sad man now, bitter at his ill health and sometimes taking it out on his wife. But Marian was strong, not one to yield or even weep—not often, anyway. Nor would she give up this ranch that she and Ned had built, even though now that meant running the ranch almost entirely by herself.

Protecting the ranch, too. Which was why she was so interested when she saw a figure dart into her barn moments earlier. A man, running right in the midst of the storm . . .

Very odd. Why would anyone do that? This had not been someone merely dodging out of the storm—he had run like a man terrified. Why was anyone out on foot in the night, anyway? And mixed in with the thunder—had that been shots she'd heard from somewhere far out in the darkness?

Marian's life was quite isolated; she had only meager contact with neighbors, all of whom lived miles away. She knew nothing of the camp meeting going on over near Woodhawk. She had not heard of the death of the blacksmith, nor indeed of any of the depredations of Henry Kidd, outlaw. She had not even heard the name. The talk of the land did not often reach her. She was an odd and offputting woman to many, and most left her alone and did not seek her out for gossip and the sharing of news.

She went to Ned's bedside and spoke to him, though she knew he would give her no indication as to whether he heard her. "I'm going to go check on something in the barn," she said. "I'll be back shortly."

He stared without blinking at the ceiling above him, as if it was her fault he was sick and he was mad at her for it. It made her angry sometimes when he did this, but lately she'd begun to suspect that he truly did not always hear her. Part of his illness, she had concluded. He was drifting away from her by the day, cut off from her most of the time.

She went to the closet and quietly took out the shotgun she kept there, always loaded. She checked it just to make sure it was, then slipped on her coat and hat and headed out the front door and around to the barn.

Join the Western Book Club and GET 4 FREE* BOOKS NOW!
A $19.96 VALUE!

Yes! I want to subscribe to the Western Book Club.

Please send me my **4 FREE* BOOKS**. I have enclosed $2.00 for shipping/handling. Each month I'll receive the four newest Leisure Western selections to preview for 10 days. If I decide to keep them, I will pay the Special Members Only discounted price of just $3.36 each, a total of $13.44, plus $2.00 shipping/handling ($22.30 US in Canada). This is a **SAVINGS OF AT LEAST $6.00** off the bookstore price. There is no minimum number of books I must buy, and I may cancel the program at any time. In any case, the **4 FREE* BOOKS** are mine to keep.

*In Canada, add $5.00 shipping/handling per order for the first shipment. For all future shipments to Canada, the cost of membership is $22.30 US, which includes shipping and handling. (All payments must be made in US dollars.)

NAME: _____

ADDRESS: _____

CITY: _____ STATE: _____

COUNTRY: _____ ZIP: _____

TELEPHONE: _____

E-MAIL: _____

SIGNATURE: _____

If under 18, Parent or Guardian must sign. Terms, prices, and conditions subject to change. Subscription subject to acceptance. Dorchester Publishing reserves the right to reject any order or cancel any subscription.

The Best in Western writing!
Get Four Books FREE*–
A $19.96 VALUE!

CHAPTER EIGHTEEN

One thing Starky Kidd had not counted on:
Rolph Knutsen's corpse falling upon him after
he shot him. As he struggled to free himself
from the limp, heavy body, he cursed himself
for not having anticipated this. Positioned as he
was, firing upward just as his attacker lunged
forward to shoot down on him, it was inevitable
that the body would plunge down right atop
him.

He struggled beneath the dead man's weight,
shoving at his bleeding body with everything he
had, and having quite a lot of trouble getting
him off. And the worst was, the falling body had
knocked his pistol out of his hand, and it lay
somewhere down in the black rock crevice into
which he was wedged.

And even now, the second manhunter—the

one who kept saying "Rolph! Rolph!"—was approaching. Coming up on almost the same spot as had this first one . . . the one named Rolph, Starky presumed.

He swore again, because it was fast becoming evident he wasn't going to be able to wiggle out from under this dead man in time. The other would be above and upon him, and there would be nothing Starky could do to defend himself.

But wait . . . His hand brushed something. The butt of a pistol, strapped into the holster worn by the dead man who was all but crushing the breath out of him. He was so wedged as to be barely able to reach it. . . .

"Rolph? Rolph, answer me! Are you all right?"

Starky strained, managed to get his hand around the butt of the pistol. He pulled, but it held in place. A leather strap, across the thumb grip of the hammer—Starky tugged at it, but it held tight. He tried again, again. . . . His thumb was unable to angle itself correctly to slip the leather strip.

"Rolph?"

The man was just above him now. Starky gave a hard, wrenching pull and the leather strip snapped. The pistol came free.

And somehow, in the same action, Starky managed to finally shift the dead Rolph into a position that let him wriggle out from beneath him. His breath coming hard, Starky wormed and writhed. . . .

* * *

York knew something was wrong. Rolph wasn't answering him, yet neither was there any noise from Kidd, other than some movement down among the rocks.

At least one of them was alive. . . . God above, let it be Rolph!

York edged toward the crevice. The lightning was less now, farther away, but still sizzling and bright. A flash in the distance cast a clear electric brilliance across the stony hillside, just in time to let York see the figure that burst up out of the crevice, pistol leveling. . . .

The pistol was unfamiliar and kicked harder than what Starky was accustomed to, but it did the job nicely. He had emptied three bullets into the new intruder even before the man could squeeze his own trigger.

The man teetered on his feet there at the edge, his form barely discernible to Starky, outlined vaguely against the sky. A lightning bolt revealed him clearly for a moment, though, and in anticipation of this possibility, Starky had put a wicked grin on his face.

"Don't you go falling on me, too," he said to the man even as he died on his feet.

York Knutsen accommodated Starky's request. He fell backward, sliding down the rocks and coming to rest unseen somewhere in a rainwater-filled natural basin at the bottom of the hill.

Starky Kidd climbed the rest of the way out of the crevice and clambered across the rocks, a happy man now, for he had again overcome the odds. Two men looking for him, two dead. Served them right!

"Rolph?" he muttered to himself, imitating York's accent. "Where are you, Rolph?" Then he laughed.

Lightning flashed across the sky, illuminating the entire landscape.

Starky Kidd sucked in his breath. There was another man, a third one! He was coming up the slope toward him—and froze when he saw Starky.

The two stood there a moment, paralyzed by surprise. A lightning flash gave them each a good look at each other.

For Starky, this was a revealing moment. As soon as he clearly saw the face of the third man, he knew he'd seen that face before. Twice, in fact, not close up . . . but he'd seen him. And that odd rifle, too, the one in his hands right now.

This man was pursuing him. Over many miles and many months. And now here they were, within yards of each other.

Starky raised his pistol and aimed it at the place the man had been. He thumbed back the hammer, but a new flash showed him . . . nothing. The man was gone! It was so swift and thorough a disappearance that Starky was for a moment uncertain that he'd actually seen a man there at all. Maybe it had been a trick of the light, or his own mind.

Then came a gunshot, and Starky Kidd fell

with a yelp, hand groping toward the side of his head. He felt a wound, blood gushing . . .

Dear God, he'd been shot! The boyish-looking fellow had dropped, rolled, and pinched off a shot with that revolver-style rifle.

Starky screeched in a high-pitched voice and staggered back. He stumbled, fell, and in so doing avoided losing his life, for a second slug sang just above him after he went down.

Terrified, head going numb around the wound, blood dripping down the side of his head and through his fingers, Starky scrambled up and ran deeper into the rocks.

Though he'd reacted quickly and well to finding himself face-to-face with Kidd, Marsh had been just as taken aback as Kidd had been. All this time, all those miles, and finally it had happened. The pair had looked into each other's eyes, and known each other. Marsh could tell, even in that brief lightning-light illumination. Kidd had recognized him. If he didn't know his name, he'd known his face, and why he was there.

The two prior times that Marsh had gotten within view of Kidd, he'd wondered if Kidd had seen him in turn. That look of recognition on Kidd's face gave him his answer.

It ends tonight, he thought. *He's in my grasp now, and I'll not see morning before I see him go down.*

He ran up the hill, following directly after the fleeing Kidd.

CHAPTER NINETEEN

Marian Stevenson entered the barn slowly, shotgun ready and senses on alert. Since the time she'd left the house she'd heard other shots out in the darkness, some distance away but too close to be casual about. And the pattern of fire indicated a fight of some sort.

She moved into the dark barn and immediately backed into a corner. Holding her breath, she listened closely. Her eyes narrowed and she felt puzzled.

Gathering her courage, she advanced slowly, trying to make little noise but of course failing to do so. She headed toward a nearby stall.

"Who's in there?" she demanded. "I know you're in there—and I've got a shotgun I'll use!"

"I need some help—he's hurt!" The voice was

plaintive and childish, in a way, though it was obviously the voice of a man.

"I'm opening this door . . . you don't move a muscle!" she ordered.

A battered lantern hung on a nail driven into a beam. Nervously, she dug a block of matches from her pocket and lit the lantern, feeling vulnerable because during that lighting she wasn't in real control of the shotgun. But the man in the stable did not emerge or do anything threatening. But she did hear, to her surprise, a canine whimper.

The lantern flooded light through the barn. She opened the door of the stall and thrust the lantern forward.

"Dear Lord," she said. "What in the world is happening here?"

Starky Kidd was ready when his pursuer came around the stone. He fired off a quick shot that almost struck him in the head, but the fellow ducked back just in time. The bullet sang off into the storm, which was now beginning to wane a little.

"Who are you!" Kidd bellowed. "I've seen your ugly face before!"

"My name's Marsh Perkins, Kidd! I've tracked you for many a mile, and tonight I'll end your trail for good!"

"You're messing with the wrong man! I'll leave your corpse cut up for the crows to eat!"

Marsh took a shot at him, missed. Kidd yelled in fury and returned fire. His shot sang high.

Marsh scrambled for cover, difficult to do in the darkness and on rain-slickened rocks. Kidd took another shot and missed again.

"You remember the war, Kidd? Remember them you killed and cut on back in North Carolina? Their people ain't forgot! I've been sent to kill you, and I will!"

"Damn you!" He took another shot, this time aiming so wide that Marsh could tell he really didn't know where he was.

"I'm taking your scarred hand back to show the others," Marsh said. "That way they'll know that you're dead!"

Kidd roared in fury. Marsh realized that the man probably was not at all used to being taunted. Normally he was in the position of power, probably mocking those he murdered. To have someone throw defiance in his face infuriated him.

Good. A man out of control is a man more easily tripped up. Marsh promised himself to bring this quest to an end tonight.

Kidd yelled, "I'm bleeding here, you bastard! You've done shot me, and I don't let nobody do that!"

"Come get me!" Marsh yelled back.

He heard Kidd moving. He was looking for him. But Marsh would give him no further clues. He was through throwing words back and forth. From now on, silence—let Kidd grow puzzled, and nervous. And, with luck, careless.

"Where are you, fool! What did you say your

name was? Perkins? Come out like a man if you want to fight me!"

Marsh held quiet. Let Kidd come to him.

"Where are you, coward? You afraid of me all at once?"

Marsh hardly breathed. Kidd was coming closer.

"What the hell's wrong with you? Come out and fight!"

Closer yet. Marsh got ready. In only a moment he should be able to confront Kidd at point-blank range.

"Damn you, show yourself!"

From out in the darkness somewhere, another voice sounded. "Marsh! Is that you?"

Marsh could have dropped where he stood. Serandon! Of all times for him to appear!

"Who the hell—" Kidd wheeled.

"Mr. Serandon—get away from here!" Marsh yelled, though he despised revealing his location so close to Kidd. "Kidd is here! Get away!"

"I'll not leave you here alone!" Serandon hollered. "I'll be up to help you!"

Marsh came out from his hiding place, ready now to take on Kidd whether from an advantageous position or otherwise. Serandon would either run Kidd off or get himself killed.

But Kidd was gone. He'd simply disappeared. Marsh was left puzzled. He heard movement below—Serandon climbing up.

What if Kidd had gone down after him?

"Mr. Serandon!" Marsh yelled, oblivious now to his own danger. "Get away, fast!"

"Well, Perkins, looks like old Starky won this one," a voice said.

Marsh turned. Kidd was just behind him, pistol up, finger squeezing down. . . .

Marsh did the only thing he could and flung himself back, off the rocks on which he stood. He did not know whether he would strike an embankment or plunge off a bluff. The move, though, saved him from Kidd's bullet. It sang above him even as he fell.

Half a moment later he struck hard, rough stone and fell, rolling. Blackness engulfed him. He twisted, a half-turn, then struck water that immersed him in cold darkness. He lost all perception of direction and location. His rifle, in his hand earlier, now was gone.

Marsh splashed and flailed, and a few moments later his head broke the surface of inky water and he gulped in air. He was in deep blackness, only a circle of relatively brighter blackness above him to give him any point of perception. Rain peppered onto his face as he looked up.

He'd plunged into a pit, or sinkhole, or oddly angled cavern. It was full of water—moving water, he noticed. An underground stream, perhaps existing only after hard storms like the current one.

The water was rising. Panic threatened; if it rose too high and he couldn't make his way out, he could drown. But if he made his way out now, Kidd would be up there, waiting for him. . . .

A dark figure loomed above, partially obscuring the hole. Marsh reacted just in time, sucking in air and pulling himself beneath the water's surface, clambering down by pulling himself down the rough, submerged wall. He heard the shots from above through the muffling water roaring in his ears, and was aware of the slugs zipping through the water beside him. But he had pulled himself back beneath a submerged overhang, and as long as he was here, Kidd could not find an angle to shoot him.

He wondered how long he could hold his breath. To get his next breath he would have to break water at the same exposed place as before. Kidd would be waiting, and shoot him as soon as he appeared.

He held his breath as long as he could, mentally voiced the prayer of a man about to die, and kicked his way back out and up.

When his head came through the surface of the water, no shots sounded. But there was commotion above, voices, shouts, the sound of a struggle.

Something large and dark plunged into the hole and down toward Marsh. He barely had time to suck in a breath before he was driven deep beneath the water, pinned there by the heavy thing that had struck him. He struggled to free himself, but could not. His lungs began to ache for air, his vision to fill with bursting stars. He was trapped beneath cold water, and passing out . . .

The blackness claimed him just as his lungs

lost their ability to hold air. In moments, he would breathe, filling his chest with water.

It would be over soon. He ceased struggling, and with his last flickering consciousness he readied himself to die.

CHAPTER TWENTY

"Ah! You are still with us, I see. Very good!"

Marsh blinked, opening his eyes. He squeezed them closed again, though, as light assaulted them. He groaned, winced violently, then very slowly opened them again.

He managed to hold them open this time. He saw a cloudy, gray sky, dim with either evening or morning light. Then, moving into his field of vision from one side, a face appeared, smiling down on him.

"I feared you would never wake up," Juan Carlos said. "God was with you, my friend. In a hundred different ways you could have died between the time you went into that pit and the time I found you. Yet you live."

Marsh groaned, then asked, "How did you find me?"

"I heard the sounds of the fight in the night, from some distance. I came, but no one remained. No sign of anything beyond a few spent cartridges I found among the rocks. Then, when the sun rose, I found the pit, and in it, you. And the other man, too, may God rest his soul."

Marsh began to remember. His last consciousness was of being pushed beneath the water by something heavy, something he could get out from under. He remembered his final prayer, and his expectation of drowning.

"How did I survive?"

"I can't know," Carlos replied. "It appears you floated to the surface of the water, and managed to drag yourself into a place that held your body in place after you passed out. Your face was barely above the surface."

"How did you get me out?"

"A rope. And muscle. It was not easy, my amigo."

"Thank you for saving me."

"I accept your thanks. I only regret I could not save the other man."

"Other man . . ."

"Yes. In the pit with you, a corpse, floating. I was able to fish it out. It lies yonder. God rest his soul."

Kidd? Could it be? Marsh remembered the sound of struggle above the mouth of the pit. Maybe Serandon had been gotten the advantage of Kidd while he was distracted. Maybe the dark and heavy thing that had plunged into the pit and pinned him down had been the corpse of Henry Kidd.

Marsh managed to sit up. Carlos said, "Perhaps you should—"

Marsh waved him off. "I want to see that dead man."

Carlos reached down, lent him a hand as he rose. Marsh shook his head slowly, blinking, and managed to find his balance. He coughed a few times.

"The unfortunate man is over here," Carlos said.

Marsh walked over and looked down at the body. Carlos had laid it out in dignified fasion, on its back, hands crossed over the chest. Two of the fingers were broken, Marsh noticed, probably during the fall into the pit.

He hadn't known Serandon well, in fact had been somewhat annoyed by him, but he'd known him to be a good man. It would be difficult to tell his wife and daughter that he was gone.

Marsh looked into the face of his dead former companion and vowed again that the one responsible for this would pay.

"I had hoped it would be Henry Kidd," Marsh said sadly.

"Sí," said Carlos. "The day Henry Kidd dies will be a blessed day for this world."

Marsh looked at Carlos's handsome face. "You know about Henry Kidd, do you?"

"I know much about him. I have been tracking him since he left Mexico."

"Kidd was in Mexico?"

"For several years. At the cost of several lives."

"I've been tracking him, too."

"I know. I know all about you, Marsh Perkins."

Marsh stared at Carlos, astonished. "But how?"

"When a man follows a trail that another also follows, it does not take long for him to find that other person. I began to detect you quite some time back. And from those few along the way who learned of your quest, I was able to learn much about you. As much, anyway, as can be gleaned in such a fashion."

"Tell me what you know."

"I know you are Marshall Perkins, a young man from North Carolina who has come to Texas on the trail of Henry Kidd, who killed several in your home area many years ago. Is my information correct?"

"It is. But you have the advantage. I know nothing about you."

"We shall have to change that, no? Especially if we are to work together."

"Work together?"

"It makes sense, does it not? You and I together can do more than we can apart. If we are to ride the same trail, we should do so together."

"I don't know you. I don't know if I can trust you."

"I saved your life. Does that count for nothing?"

"It counts for much. But I can't do anything that would endanger my quest."

"I understand fully. I would not ask you to do that."

"Who are you, then?"

"To most I meet, I am a traveling writer, in Texas to follow the outlaw Henry Kidd and tell about his depredations. There is much interest in him in Mexico. He entered Mexico after your great war, and killed several innocent people. Afterward, he vanished for a year, then appeared again, some miles away. Still killing. Still the diablo. Among those he killed was my brother. He cut his throat, then damaged his body in ways that are shameful even to describe."

"It's always his way to do that."

"I vowed that one day I would find this Henry Kidd and see justice done to him. So you see, our quests are much the same, and as different as we are, we are much alike."

"Yes. But there's one difference: It will be me, and not you, who kills Henry Kidd."

"How do you know this?"

"My grandmother had a vision about it."

Marsh waited for Carlos to laugh, but he did not. "I knew a woman once with the same gift," he said. "She was old and wise, and I missed her when she died. She was the mother of my wife."

"You left a wife behind to chase Henry Kidd?"

"No. My wife is gone. I buried her a year ago."

"I'm sorry." A dreadful possibility came to mind. "Mr. Carlos . . . the death of your wife . . . it wasn't . . ."

"No. It was not Kidd. She died naturally. But it was only after she died that I was free to begin pursuing him, as I had vowed to do."

"Are you in fact a writer?"

"Yes, and the day will come when I will tell the story of this quest, and its fulfillment."

Marsh looked down at the corpse of Serandon, a man who had died trying to save him. It was difficult to keep his emotions in check. "When you write that story, this will be one of the sad parts. This man was named Serandon. He has a wife and daughter. They are at the camp meeting some distance from here. And I'll have to ride to it and tell them news that will destroy them."

"It is the legacy of Starky Kidd, no?"

Marsh looked quickly at Carlos. "Starky?" Something triggered in his mind. Among the last things Kidd had said to him . . . he had used the name "Starky" in reference to himself.

"Why did you call him Starky just now?"

Carlos looked seriously at Marsh. "I had come to believe that you did not know the full truth about who you are tracking. It took much time and thought for me to surmise it myself."

"Are you telling me that Henry Kidd is not Henry Kidd?"

"As you perceive Henry Kidd, that is exactly what I am telling you."

Marsh sat down, hands on the side of his head, and slumped forward. This was all too much to deal with. A man who had tried to assist him had gotten killed for his efforts. Kidd had escaped once more. And now it appeared that the very premise upon which Marsh had based his quest was not correct.

"Talk to me," he said to Carlos. "I want to know all you can tell me."

CHAPTER TWENTY-ONE

Starky Kidd touched the aching wound on his head left by the grazing shot fired by Marsh Perkins. He cursed the fellow, whoever he was—or had been—and hoped his death down in that pit had been slow and hard.

He was rather proud of the idea of having tossed the other man's body into the pit—an idea inspired by his own experience in that rocky crevice when the body had fallen atop him.

He even had a prize from the night before: the interesting revolver-style rifle carried by that baby-faced North Carolina manhunter, Perkins. He'd lost it when he fell into the hole, and Starky had retrieved it. He'd enjoy toying around with it later, when there was time and he was at some safer place.

Starky's happiness at his own survival and diabolical cleverness was muted, though, by his worries about Henry. His brother was gone. Starky had returned to the cave in which he'd left him, but Henry had vanished. The horses remained, along with their meager personal possessions, but no Henry.

So now Starky Kidd was a man with a problem. He desperately needed to flee these parts, especially now that he'd added even more murders to his history, but he couldn't leave without his brother. Family loyalty had a degree of hold even in his black soul, but more than that, he feared what Henry might reveal. In his half-witted innocence he might give away the locations of the places in which they roamed and hid, or present some crucial clue that would assure the gallows for Starky.

He had to find Henry. But how? The storm had washed away all tracks.

"Think, Starky!" he muttered to himself. "Try to think like Henry—why would you have run out in a storm that way? 'Specially with the lightning going so hard. Because of the shooting?"

It was the only possibility he could think of. The sound of the gun battle might have drawn him out. Either that, or something in the cave had frightened him out. But Starky was relatively sure the cave had been free of animal occupants when they entered it. Maybe something wandered in during the storm, seeking refuge.

But once out of the cave, where would Henry

have gone? He hadn't returned. Maybe something had happened to him. Maybe there were other pits like the one Marsh Perkins had fallen into.

Starky rode down a swollen creek, leading Henry's riderless horse behind his, hiding their tracks in the water, going nowhere in particular, just moving because it was his compulsion. Yet he wouldn't leave, not yet. Not until he'd found Henry again.

Where would Henry have gone? And why? He racked his brain . . . and then a possibility arose.

Starky thought it over and nodded. It was the only likely possibility he could think of. There was really no other place in the vicinity that Henry would have gone. He should have thought of it right away.

He guided the horses out of the creek and turned toward the northeast.

Back among the rocks that had been stage to all the violence of the prior night, Marsh Perkins sat listening to Juan Carlos as the mystery of Henry Kidd slowly clarified a little in his mind. Links were clicking together, murky experiences becoming clear.

"It's amazing," Marsh said, having heard Carlos's information. "I feel a right fool for having never figured it out myself. I've been trailing two men, not one—all this time, two men. It takes away any pride I had in my tracking skills."

"Don't be critical of yourself," Carlos said. "It took me a long while to figure it out myself. Starky Kidd is an adept man in his own wicked way. Simpleminded, yet fiendishly clever in terms of his ability to hide his tracks and activities. He has hidden away the real Henry Kidd for years, keeping him as it were in his pocket, close by but out of sight of all others."

" 'Fiendishly clever,' " Marsh repeated. "That's the truth. Living as one man, but committing his crimes using the name of his brother. Shifting the blame, so that if ever the trap springs, maybe it would spring on Henry instead of him. I'd have never figured such a thing out if you hadn't come along. I thank you."

"You would have come to the same conclusion over time," Carlos said. "If you think back, I suspect there are times along the way that you've encountered situations that will make more sense when you reconsider them with the knowledge that you have been trailing two men rather than one."

Marsh nodded. "There were such times," he said. "They seemed hard to account for . . . until now. Once, when I was very close on the trail, I noticed the tracks of two horses rather than one. But I dismissed it as Henry Kidd riding one horse and leading a packhorse. I guess it wasn't a packhorse after all. And twice I encountered people who told me of meeting a man named Henry Kidd, and they described him as kind, gentle . . . simple. I just dismissed those people as having made some sort of mistake. The Henry Kidd I was following wouldn't have helped an old woman fix the broken wheel of her wagon. He wouldn't have carried a little boy with a broken ankle back to his home, carrying him for nearly a mile on a hot day, so that his family could get him to the nearest doctor. I heard these tales of a kindly Henry Kidd from time to time, but I couldn't make them fit the man as I knew him. So I just put them down for mistakes or misidentifications. There have always been some people eager to paint a good face on outlaws and scoundrels, anyway. Makes for good legends." He paused. "Are you absolutely certain that what you say is true, Mr. Carlos? There are, without any question, two Kidd brothers?"

"It is true. I know it to be so, because I once met the real Henry Kidd."

"Face-to-face?"

"Indeed. And at the time I had no idea to whom I was speaking. I found him alone in a hidden camp, a simple, homely, friendly fellow who seemed to welcome my company. I noted he seemed to resemble the man I was tracking, the one who in my mind at that time was Henry Kidd—this was not the same man. He was friendly, but nervous, waiting for the return of his brother, whom he called Starky. He did not say his own name; I believe now that he'd been instructed not to reveal it. I talked briefly with him, gave him some smoked meat I carried with me, then went on my way. Later, I learned there had been a murder and mutilation on a farm about two miles from that location, about the same time I was talking to the simple fellow in the camp. It bore all the usual marks of a Kidd murder. Then there came a report from a boy who saw two men riding away from the area, one of them with a description exactly matching that of the man to whom I had given the smoked meat."

"But how do you know he is the real Henry Kidd?"

"I learned it from a drunkard in a small town near the border. He is one of the few who have encountered Starky Kidd and come away from the experience alive. Others dismissed his story, but I believe it. He claims he drank with Starky Kidd one night in a little cantina, and that Starky revealed the entire affair to him—his true name, his use of his brother's name in association with his crimes, his scheme to have his innocent brother pay the penalty for him if ever they are caught. Have you not thought it odd that this killer has always taken pains to make sure the name 'Henry Kidd' has been left behind at the scenes of his crimes? How many murderers leave behind their names, sometimes written in the blood of their victims?"

"Or even carved into their flesh a time or two."

"Yes. I have heard that, too."

"But why would Starky have revealed so much to this drunk?"

"He was drunk himself at the time. And I believe his intention was to kill the fellow afterward. But he drank too much and passed out. The other one simply slipped away."

Marsh thought it over. "If there are two Kidd brothers, where was the real Henry last night?"

"Somewhere nearby, I am sure. By now his brother has undoubtedly retrieved him and they have moved on. I anticipate that Starky will leave this region now. There has been too much activity for him to feel sufficiently safe to remain here."

"It's the usual pattern. A few killings within fifty or sixty square miles of territory, then he moves on. Yes, I think you're right. He'll be leaving the territory now."

"Which means we must find the trail soon."

"Yes."

"What next, then?"

Marsh paused. "There is one thing I must do right away. Mr. Serandon's body must be returned to his family. I dread it deeply."

"I'll go with you," Carlos said. "I'll help you out. From now on, until our common quest is done, I propose that it be that way: I help you, you help me. Agreed?" He thrust out his hand.

Marsh, for all the time he'd been on the trail, had never envisioned taking on a partner. It was in his nature to work alone, and his quest was so unique and private that he'd never anticipated encountering anyone else following almost the identical path. But he liked Juan Carlos, and trusted him instinctively. Thanks to what he'd learned, he understood much better just who he was pursuing. So with no hesitation, he shook Carlos's hand.

"Agreed," he said.

CHAPTER TWENTY-TWO

Marian Stevenson walked to her husband's bedside, looking at him in the light of morning streaming through the window. He was asleep now, or so she felt reasonably sure; it was often hard to tell, given the effects of the strange, debilitating disease that controlled both his body and mind. She looked by lamplight down into his face, and spoke to him even though she doubted he heard, understood, or cared.

"There is another man here tonight, dear," she said softly. "I found him in the barn, in a stall, hugging a dog that had been hurt in the lightning and had run to hide in the barn. Just like he had himself. He seems such a tender soul . . . but he isn't right in his mind. He's very slow, not smart. But so kind! He was so tender with that poor dog. Just like you were back when we were young, always tender toward hurt animals."

She stroked her husband's brow and gave him an unseen smile. "I miss you, Ned. When you are aware, you are sad and angry and won't speak to me. When you are not aware, just lost in your world, wherever that is, you are out of reach to me. It's as if you are gone already sometimes." She reached up and wiped away a tear. "I'm glad that the young man has come. It's good to have someone here who is kind and tender. But I think he's ill. He's coughed a lot, and he doesn't look well. And I don't know why a man so simpleminded would be alone. He talks about a brother who takes care of him, but he doesn't know where he is. Maybe he will come to find him. I don't know. Henry's sleeping now. It was hard for him to go to sleep, though. He was very upset. The poor dog didn't survive."

She looked at her unresponsive husband a minute more, in silence. It crossed her mind that it was not only her new visitor who seemed sickly. Ned himself had an odd pallor and his breathing was slower than usual. He was sleeping very, very deeply.

"Oh, Ned," she whispered, because she sensed a time might be fast approaching that she had long dreaded. "Oh, Ned, please grow stronger. Don't go away and leave me here even more alone than I am now!"

She leaned over and kissed him, then pulled up a cane-bottomed chair near the bed, sat down on it, and pulled a comforter across her lap. Then she simply sat, staring at her husband and wishing things were different than they were.

For Marsh, the ride to the camp meeting site was slow and silent. Carlos talked about the Kidd brothers, seemingly unmoved by the fact that they were carrying a dead man's body on a dragging litter attached to the back of Marsh's horse. Marsh wondered if the man was hard-hearted, but reminded himself that Carlos had not known Serandon at all. He had not seen his wife and lovely daughter, and did not have to dread, as Marsh did, what it would be like to share with them the terrible news.

As they neared the campsite and heard the swell of a hymn being sung, though, Carlos apparently sensed Marsh's feelings. He went silent for a time and grow somber.

"This will be a difficult moment for you, eh, amigo?" he asked.

"Yes. He had a wife and beautiful daughter, both of whom believe he is still alive and well and helping me search for a murderer. They believe right now that their husband and father is a hero."

"And so he is."

"Yes. But a dead one. And dead heroes cannot hug their daughters and kiss their wives."

"Come, my friend. Let's go on and get this done. It is hard to share bad news, but I'll be beside you."

Marsh nodded. At the moment he was glad to have a partner, any partner, at his side.

Noon. On a typical day, Marian Stevenson would be preparing a simple meal for her silent husband and herself. Today she had not even thought of food. She was growing more alarmed by the moment.

Someone came to the door of the room, making her turn with a gasp. She had become so preoccupied by her husband's fast-declining health that she had actually forgotten Henry Kidd was in the house.

"Henry . . . you scared me."

"I'm sorry. I didn't mean to." He looked at Ned. "Is he your father?"

"No. He's my husband."

"He looks too old for that."

"He is older than I am. But he is also very sick."

Henry stared at him and coughed deeply. Marian said, "Henry, I think you're sick, too. A different kind. How long have you coughed that way?"

"I cough a lot. This whole year I've coughed a whole lot. My brother, he says, 'Quit that coughing!' But I cough anyway, because I can't help it."

"Do you have any idea where your brother is?"

"No. He's just out there. Somewhere."

"Will he come to get you?"

"I don't know where he is. I guess he don't know where I am."

"Is he good to you, Henry?" She had her doubts that he was good. Henry had been so filled with fear when she first found him, unwilling even to reveal his name without an hour of prodding, that she knew he had suffered in his day.

"He gives me food. He gets me clothes and such when I need new ones. He lets me stay with him."

"He's a good man, then?"

Henry's face darkened. He would not look at her. "I don't think he is. I think he may be a bad man."

"Henry, will he come here, do you think?"

"I don't think he will." He looked worried. "How can I get with him again? I don't know where to look for him!" Then he coughed some more, deeper than before.

"It was bad for you to be wet in the storm last night. It's made you ill. You should go to bed and stay warm. I'm going to go fetch someone who will help you. And Ned. I think both of you need a doctor."

"I've never seen no doctor. Not ever."

"The man I'm thinking of isn't a real doctor, either. But he's as good as one, most times. He has a talent for helping the sick." But she looked at her weakly breathing husband and doubted that any doctor, even a highly trained, authentic one, could do much for him now.

She did not allow herself even to mentally

voice the words, but she knew Ned was dying. It made her sad but also furious. It was wrong that a man could die of so strange a malady, an illness that ate away both body and mind and sent folks to their graves without even a name for their loved ones to attach to the ailment that killed them.

"Don't leave," Henry pleaded. "When Starky left, I couldn't find him anymore."

She thought a few moments, eyes narrowing. "I heard shooting out in the darkness last night, off some in the distance. Could any of it have been your brother shooting?"

"I don't know. I thought maybe it was. I heard the shooting too, and went out to see. But I got scared of the lightning—lightning is real bad to me—and I just ran. I ran and ran and ran until I found your barn. And there was the poor dog inside, all hurt and crying." Henry's eyes began to moisten and grow red. He coughed hard, and made a face that showed it hurt.

"You go to bed, Henry. I'm going to fetch Joe Parker. He's the man who helps sick people. I think you're ill, Henry . . . and I'm afraid my husband might be dying."

CHAPTER TWENTY-THREE

Bounty hunters. Starky Kidd had learned to spot them long ago. You could always tell. Sometimes he could all but smell it on them.

This was a big band. Four of them, encamped together. He actually recognized one of them, a big fellow who had tracked him and Henry for two days before Starky could figure out a way to give him the slip. There was a second one, too, who looked vaguely familiar. Maybe he'd tracked him too, at one time or another.

He was hiding in the rocks, not far from that pit into which the baby-faced tracker out of North Carolina had fallen, and into which Starky had thrown the body of the other man he'd killed. It was odd indeed to be stuck at such a place, and it had not been his intention to get into such a situation. It's just that the sorry bounty hunters had camped themselves in such a place that he now could not come out without being seen. The unwitting idiots had trapped him and didn't even know it.

Starky always followed a rule when it came to bounty hunters: When they start showing up in bunches, it's time to strike off for new territory.

He was ready to do that. He'd not leave Texas, not right away, but he'd go to another part of it. That was the good thing about Texas: It was big. A man could lose himself in it.

Right now, though, he'd do nothing but sit tight, hiding in these rocks and waiting for the bounty hunters to move on. He could be here for hours, maybe even into the night, depending on what they did. He cursed and thought himself a most unfortunate man. It was important to get away from here, but he couldn't do it without Henry, and he couldn't get to the place he thought Henry would be as long as these bounty hunters hung around.

He settled himself as comfortably as possible, hoped his horse would not make too much noise, and tried to be patient—because that's all he could do.

The storm had done much damage at the camp meeting site, tearing down the arbor above the speaking platform, whipping down makeshift tents, turning wagon ruts into small rivers and low-lying areas into ponds. Yet the people had not scattered. They'd stuck it out, and still the preaching and singing had gone on.

It was not going on now. The grim word had spread through the camp: Mr. Serandon had been murdered! It had brought to a halt all music, all preaching. The praying went on, though, grieving prayers, wails of sorrow and bitter anger sent up to the heavens from a people who had seen one killing too many.

Bailey Jones happened to be the first who had spotted Marsh and Carlos bringing in the dead body. This was unfortunate. He raced up, saw the corpse on the litter, and rushed back to the camp shouting the terrible news well before Marsh and Carlos could provide any explanation.

Thus, from the outset, the news ran out of control, unguided by facts and bolstered by speculative answers to the inevitable questions. Serandon is dead! How did he die? Henry Kidd . . . it was Henry Kidd!

Carlos had explained the true facts to the Reverend Cacey, telling him about Starky Kidd, but Cacey barely seemed to grasp it. Since the sheriff had sent him and his "army" sneaking back to the camp meeting with tails neatly tucked between legs, Cacey was deflated and dejected. He listened to the truth about Henry Kidd and the revelation of the existence of Starky Kidd, but didn't seem much interested. He did not mount the pulpit to share the truth with the others— and now it was too late. No one was listening to anything but rumors at this point.

So, like a fire in dry brush, the fury spread

through the camp meeting, uncontrolled and growing, becoming more exaggerated and inaccurate by the minute.

Marsh knew it was happening but was too preoccupied to ponder it. He focused on only one thing: Corinne Serandon and her mother, huddled together, weeping, friends trying vainly to console them. It hurt to see it. He felt partly responsible for their bereavement.

What hurt most of all was that Corinne, the admired girl he had never met and now probably never would, apparently held him responsible as well. She had turned a few moments before and glared at him with obvious hatred. He had been the one whom her father had followed out to look for Kidd. It was he whom Serandon had died trying to save. He was the reason her father was dead!

Marsh wanted to vanish. Just close his eyes and go off into some oblivion. He didn't care about Starky Kidd, Henry Kidd, or his quest. The cost was just too high. It was too much for him.

Carlos came to him and grasped his shoulder, rather hard. Marsh looked up at him.

"What is this?" Carlos said sternly. "Do I see you trying to hold back tears? Listen, amigo, there is no time for pitying yourself. Do you know what is happening here?"

"What do you mean?"

"What is happening here is wrong. The rumor is sweeping through this entire camp that Henry Kidd is responsible for the death of Serandon. We were fools, you and I, to bring the body in as we did. We should have gone first to the preacher and told him the story, and told him that it is Starky Kidd, and not Henry, who is the murderer. He could have told it all to this group in a way that made them understand, and then we could have broken the news about Serandon to them gently, without stirring them as they are now. Now it is too late. Look!"

Marsh looked where Carlos pointed. A group of seven men, well-armed, were riding out of the camp. Nearby, another band was saddling up.

"What are they doing?" Marsh asked numbly. His brain seemed to be functioning slowly right now.

"What do you think? They are going to find and kill Henry Kidd."

"But Henry Kidd didn't kill Serandon. It was Starky."

"*Dios!* Of course we know that! But *they* don't know it! They believe, like Starky Kidd has wanted them to believe, that it is Henry who is the killer! They don't even know of the existence of Starky Kidd! We were fools, amigo, fools. We did not do this task as we should."

Marsh watched the second band ride out. The "Army of God" whose ignoble career had been cut short by a sharp-tongued sheriff and a leader with short-lived determination was now energizing again, but with a difference. This time they were dividing into small bands. This time they were truly, deeply, bitterly angry.

Marsh's nerves were raw, his body and mind tired. Temper flared. He glared at Carlos. "I don't much care whether we did it right or not," he said. "I don't even care much about Henry Kidd or Starky Kidd just now. I'm just too tired and sick to my stomach because of what happened."

"You don't *care*? What has happened to you? You've traveled your road all the way from Carolina, and now you don't care that armed men are going after an innocent man?"

"I can't help it that Henry Kidd was unfortunate enough to be born with an evil brother who is willing to betray him to save his own skin. That's not my fault, Juan Carlos. It's not your fault. None of this is our fault!"

"I am speaking less of fault than of justice, amigo. Justice. If Henry Kidd, the true and innocent Henry Kidd, is found, he will be shot down or hanged, and the true murderer might well go free. That would be a mockery. It would be Starky Kidd spitting on the graves of every person he has murdered."

"Juan, even if we could make every person here understand the truth—which we can't—what difference would it make? These people aren't the only ones searching for Henry Kidd. There are bounty hunters, lawmen, common folks guarding their families—they've all heard of Henry Kidd and know nothing of Starky."

"But *we* know. We must seek to stop the injustice, if we can."

Marsh looked over at the weeping Serandon

women and felt another pang of remorse and
guilt, even though he knew in the rational part
of his mind that he bore no fault for Serandon's
death. That thought gave rise to another,
though: If he found it painful and unfair that
Corinne Serandon held him in wrongful blame
for her father's death, was it any different for
Henry Kidd, blamed falsely for the crimes of
another?

"All right, then," Marsh said. "Very well. We
must try to set things right. But what do you
suggest we do?"

"It is not possible for us to make half a nation
suddenly understand the truth, and start blam-
ing Starky Kidd rather than Henry. We must be
the ones to find the Kidd brothers. We must destroy Starky Kidd, but protect Henry. No one
else but us will do that."

"That's a tall order."

"We are almost certain to fail. But we must
try, for the sake of justice. Remember, few people are alive who know the face of Starky Kidd,
or Henry. If the pair is caught, Starky will probably be able to persuade them that his brother
is the man they seek. He is clever enough for
that."

"How can we hope to find them?"

"We have as good a chance as any of these
armed bands—see? There goes another! Come
with me, Marsh. Let's go back to where you
fought Starky Kidd, and see if the Almighty
might bless us with clues and a successful
hunt."

"I have no rifle," Marsh said. "It was lost in the fight."

"Then we will find you one to replace it. There are plenty of them in this camp. Now let's go. I have the strongest sense that if we look now, we may be successful. God will ride with us, my friend. He will deliver Starky Kidd into our hands."

To Marsh, that sounded like the things the Reverend Cacey had said the day before as the Army of God amassed. And look how wrong he had been! But he didn't say this to Carlos. Like everything else at this moment, it just didn't seem to matter much.

CHAPTER TWENTY-FOUR

Starky Kidd, still hidden in the rocks, swore bitterly but not loudly. The band of bounty hunters was still encamped and showed no signs of being about to move, and now a whiskey bottle had been brought out and was being passed among the members of the increasingly merry group.

These men were going nowhere anytime soon. And from his higher vantage point among the rocks, Starky could see a second group of riders, three men, heading in his direction.

He couldn't remain. It was growing far too dangerous. Nothing to do but creep away, and forget for now about finding Henry.

Starky took one last look toward the place he'd been trying to reach: the ranch house whose light he'd seen in the darkness the night before, just before that wild fight for his life. He didn't know Henry was there, but it was a reasonably strong possibility. Henry had known that's where he was going. He might have gone there himself, looking for his brother.

Disappointed, dejected, and more scared than he would admit, Henry Kidd withdrew into the rocks, worked his way back to the little draw where the horses were hidden, mounted up, and rode away, leaving the rocky hills between himself and the bounty hunters.

Could he circle around toward the house from some other, safer direction? Perhaps, but it would take time and force him to ride in the open for a long distance. He hardly dared do that. Perhaps after darkness fell—if he could stay hidden that long.

Hiding held a lot of appeal. Too many people were looking for him. He had to find a place to roost where he would not be found. And it looked like he would have to do it, for the moment, anyway, without Henry.

Marian Stevenson's horse was familiar with the road to the community of Parmeter and apparently liked it, because it always traveled at a fast and efficient clip when she went there. There was not much to Parmeter, but there was a trading post from which she bought the items she could not make or find on her own. And there was Ben Rumley, the old Civil War wound dresser who now served as the closest thing this region had to a practicing physician.

Ben was a wagon maker by trade, and was hard at work on a buckboard when Marian rode up and told him about her husband's condition. Preoccupied with Ned, she did not mention Henry.

He greeted her description of Ned's decline with a grim expression. "I'll look at him, but this isn't a broken arm we're talking about here, Marian. Ned is very sick. I don't even understand the nature of his illness. I think he needs a real doctor."

"It's too late for a real doctor, Ben. I know that. And I know there is probably nothing you can do, either. But still, I owe it to Ned to do all I can. Maybe you can help me make him comfortable, if nothing else. Maybe you'll think of something unexpected that can make him better. All I ask is that you look at him."

Ben looked down at the unfinished buckboard. Going back to the Stevenson spread would throw him behind on finishing it, and the commissioner of this project was already growing impatient. But duty was duty.

"Come on," he said. "We'll take a look. Give me a moment to pull my things together."

Marian's degree of worry became clear to Ben when they were within a mile of her ranch. A band of armed riders went by on a trot, a quarter of a mile away, and she didn't seem to notice. She was pushing hard to reach the house, as if fearful that too long a delay might have a cost she did not want to pay.

Ben watched the riders disappear over a swell in the land. He was vaguely comforted to have seen them. Because of the outlaw Henry Kidd, there were many such groups ranging through this region. They were tense, trigger-happy, dangerous bands, but with such a murderer as Kidd around, Ben felt safer for their presence.

He felt a little guilty, too, when he considered that he had given no thought to the situation of Marian and her bedridden husband. Living out like they did, alone and with little contact with others, they were in a particularly precarious situation with Henry Kidd roaming around. Nobody knew how Kidd survived, so the presumption was he stole to survive. An outlying ranch whose only male occupant was disabled was a strong potential target. Ben decided he'd been amiss in not checking on the Stevensons. But the truth was that he hadn't even thought of them until Marian showed up today.

They came within view of the house. Marian seemed both relieved and anxious to be home again.

"You look worried, Marian," Ben said as he stepped onto the yard. "Are you concerned that Ned has been here alone?"

"Oh, he's not been alone," she said. "There's another man here. He's slow in his mind, but very gentle."

"I didn't know you'd hired help."

"I haven't. He just showed up. I found him in my barn and I guess just took him in."

"Who is he?"

"He says his name is Henry. Henry Kidd."

Ben jolted to a stop and froze for several moments. "My God!" he declared. Drawing his pistol, he rushed to the door, paused there . . .

"Ben, what in the world—"

He didn't wait for her to finish. He pushed the door open and burst inside, pistol drawn. No one there. He looked back toward the bedroom and saw motion.

"Ben, for God's sake, put away that pistol!" Marian said, coming in the door behind Ben.

Ben did not heed her at all. He rushed into the bedroom and again froze, astonished and appalled by the scene that met his eyes.

CHAPTER TWENTY-FIVE

"There they are," Marsh said, eyeing the rocky hills where he had endured his own violent encounter with Starky Kidd. "I'll never forget what happened among those rocks. That pit almost killed me . . . but maybe saved my life, too. If I hadn't fallen in when I did, Starky Kidd would have killed me."

"Why don't we take a look among those hills," Carlos suggested. "This is largely flat country, and Starky needs to hide. He might be drawn to these hills."

"Even after all that happened here? He may have gotten away, but he was close to disaster himself."

"One never knows. A man seeking to hide can only go to where hiding places are. Perhaps in

157

one of those caves we will find him, or at least some clue."

Marsh nodded. They had been searching for a good while, but with no luck. They'd seen other riders, but they weren't the Kidd brothers, but others like themselves, out in search of Starky—though all but Marsh and Carlos, of course, did not know of Starky and were in their own minds looking only for one Kidd, Henry. A good number of them had only hours before been among the number of Cacey's failed Army of God.

Marsh didn't say it, but he considered this nearly hopeless. This was the classic kind of situation in which Kidd was able to vanish. Marsh had seen it before, twice. Kidd killed, evoked panic, drew swarms of manhunters . . . then vanished. It happened every time. If Marsh was more superstitious, he might be tempted to attribute some sort of supernatural capabilities to Kidd.

He did not believe it likely that he and Carlos, or any of the other manhunters, would find whom they sought.

He and Carlos rode into the hills, looking around, hoping to find some track or clue. There were some fresh tracks and other indicators of the presence of someone in the hills very recently, but who could say who it was?

Though it sent a chill down his spine to be in the area of the pit that had swallowed him, Marsh looked around on the slim hope he would find his rifle. He didn't, of course, and knew that Kidd had probably taken it. It might have fallen down into the pit with him, and now be forever lost deep in that dark subterranean water.

As Marsh had anticipated, their searching led nowhere. He was discouraged by this entire process and not fully in accord with Carlos, who seemed righteously determined to make sure that the innocent Henry Kidd did not wrongly take punishment due his brother. Marsh cared . . . but he was tired. He'd traveled very far, over a long time, to reach this place. He was so sick of manhunting, he could almost consider casting it aside and heading back to North Carolina.

A time or two he'd been tempted to actually do it. The odds were he could go back home, claim that Kidd had been killed and that he knew about it, but had been hampered from bringing back the evidence of Kidd's scarred hand. In the remote North Carolina mountains, no one would probably ever learn he'd lied.

He'd toyed with the idea, but never seriously. He would know the truth if no one else did. He'd spend the rest of his days waiting for that next stray newspaper clipping or rumor from the West revealing that Kidd had murdered yet again. Then everyone would know he had lied.

There was nothing for Marsh to do but stay on the task until it was done.

They had dismounted and were walking among the rocks, Marsh halfheartedly looking for his rifle but not expecting to find it. From atop a boulder he looked across the flatlands below the hills and noted a ranch house alone in the distance.

"Juan," he said. "There's a ranch yonder. I wonder if the Kidds might have gone there. For food, to steal something, or whatever reason."

Carlos joined him atop the boulder. "Perhaps so. There is no harm in going to see, no? But let's look through these hills a while longer. I believe that Starky Kidd may yet be hiding here. So be careful, amigo."

"Get off him!" Ben yelled as he raised his pistol.

Henry Kidd, leaning across the bed with his hands upon the mouth and throat of the stricken Ned Stevenson, looked back across his shoulder at the unexpected intruder. His eyes were wide and wild, glaring, and at that moment he looked fearsome and murderous.

"Stop choking him or I'll kill you!" Ben shouted again, his finger already beginning to tighten on the trigger.

Henry Kidd reflexively ducked, his hands slipping away from Ned. Henry collapsed back onto the floor on his rump, beside the bed, and threw his hands across his face. "No!" he screamed in a high pitch. "No!"

Marian burst into the room. "What in the world—" She looked at Ned, went to his side.

"He's going to kill me!" Henry wailed.

"I ought to kill you, you murdering son of a bitch!" Ben said. "But I believe I'll just haul you in and let the law do it."

"Ben, put down the pistol," Marian ordered firmly.

"Marian, do you know who this is? Do you know all he's done and what he was doing when I came in here?"

"This is Henry Kidd, a kind young man, and I demand that you put that pistol away, Ben! What has gotten into you?"

"Henry Kidd is a murderer, Marian. Maybe you don't know about him, cut off like you are out here. He's a murderer who has killed more people than anybody even knows. He killed poor old Port McGee in his blacksmith shop. This whole countryside has been crawling with manhunters looking for him!"

. Marian took that in but couldn't quite grasp it. It was impossible to make it fit with the gentle Henry Kidd she knew.

"He was leaned over Ned, choking him, when I came in," Ben went on.

"I wasn't!" Henry declared through tears. "I wasn't! He was choking all by himself and I was trying to stop it! I was trying to save him! To save him!" Then Henry broke off into a burst of violent coughing and was able to say no more.

Marian nodded. "I believe him, Ben. That happens sometimes—you know that. Ned's throat will close down, and at times he has literally nearly choked on his own tongue. When that happens, you have to pull his tongue clear to let him breathe. I told Henry to watch for that happening, and how to deal with it when it did."

"Why are you taking this murderer's side,

Marian? There's so much you don't know. This whole part of Texas is living in fear of this bastard right now, and he's managed to convince you he's some innocent half-wit!"

"You can't be right, Ben," she said. "This young man is no murderer—I can tell you that very firmly!" In her tone, though, the vaguest flicker of doubt was beginning to form. She recalled hearing those gunshots shortly before Henry showed up at her barn.

"Marian, I have to take him in. I have no choice. If this is the same Henry Kidd that has this county in an uproar, he has to be taken to the sheriff."

"I just can't believe that . . ." She faltered away. "Henry?" she asked. "Is it true?"

"No!" he declared. "No, no, no! It's Starky who does bad things! Starky, not me!"

"Who is Starky?" Ben asked.

"My brother!"

"I've never heard of anyone named Starky Kidd. I've only heard of Henry Kidd. Marian, you take my pistol and hold it on him while I look at Ned. Then I'll take him on to the sheriff."

"There's no need to look at Ned," she said softly. Her husband's still form and half-open eyes had just caught her attention. "He's gone, Ben."

She lowered her head and wept.

Chapter Twenty-six

Two manhunters, both young, neither particularly adept at it, both of them drunk from whiskey they'd bought earlier in Woodhawk. Camped now near a little stream, they were passing the bottle back and forth, talking big talk about what they would do with their share of the reward money once they brought in the feared Kidd.

"I'm going to buy me a bunch of busted rifles, and take them to my uncle and get him to fix them, then I'll turn around and sell them," one was saying. "I know a man who did that in Arkansas, and he makes all kinds of money now selling guns. Once I get enough, I'll open me up a full gun shop. Then I'll marry Annie Prince and have me a houseful of children in no time."

"Yeah, you would. The way she looks, you'd

not be able to keep off her. You'd have a lot of children, all right."

"Don't talk about Annie that way. She's special. You can talk about other girls that way, but not Annie."

"Well . . . Mickey's in love! I always knowed you were fond toward her, but I sure didn't know you were all lovey-dovey." The speaker's voice was slurred badly, the whiskey taking its toll.

"Don't you mock, Perry. I'm serious about this."

"I won't mock. Hey, you know what I'm going to do with my share of the reward?"

"What?"

"Buy into that new saloon. Same one we got this whiskey at."

"What makes you think they'll let you?"

"I already talked to them. They said if I could get the money, I was in."

"You'll drink up all the stock."

"Reckon I might." He laughed and turned up the bottle, closing his eyes as the hot liquor drained into his mouth and down his throat.

When he opened his eyes again and lowered the bottle, he was surprised to see Mickey sitting there with blood all over the front of his shirt and a stunned look on his face. He tried to talk, but couldn't. Slowly he tipped to one side.

Perry stared up in horror at the grinning man standing behind Mickey. He had a bloodied knife in his hand. "You ever cut a throat?" he asked Perry. "It's mighty easy. Good way to dispatch a man." Starky was proud to use the word "dispatch." He considered it a ten-dollar word, like an educated man would use, and enjoyed throwing it out from time to time. He lost his smile suddenly, however. "Hey! You're spilling that whiskey! I want that!"

Perry was trying to get to his feet, but he was drunk and terrified, and Kidd had the drop on him, anyway. Starky raised Marsh Perkins's revolving rifle and fired off three rounds that sent Perry staggering back, to collapse with his face to the sky. He stared at the moon as he died.

Starky had already rescued the whiskey, not much of which was lost. He lifted the bottle to his lips and took a swallow, then swiped the back of his hand across his mouth.

"You fellers got any food?" he asked the dead men. "I'm about starved."

He dug around in their supplies and found some cold biscuits, rather dry, along with equally dried-up fried sausage, some parched corn, and a hunk of cheese gone orange instead of yellow. Not the best fare, but good enough. Starky sat by the fire of his victims and dined, talking to them as if they were still living company.

"Well, got to go, boys," he said when he'd finished the food. "I'll take the whiskey with me. Oh, and I guess I better have brother Henry leave a note."

He used the blood from the first one he'd killed to scrawl the words "Hello from Henry Kidd" on a white shirt he'd found crammed in among their supplies. He stretched it out across the ground near the fire. With his knife he did some of his usual insulting work on the bodies.

Satisfied and feeling he'd made quite a telling commentary on the bands of amateur manhunters trying to find him, Starky smiled down at his victims. "So long, boys. Got to go a ranch house yonder way and see if my brother is there. I believe he might be. If he ain't, well, I guess he and me has finally parted. Kind of sad, huh? Oh, well."

Starky Kidd selected the better of the two horses that grazed nearby and transferred the saddle from his own exhausted mount. Mounting, he rode off in the direction of the ranch house of Marian Stevenson.

Two hours later, in the deep of night, Carlos stood outside the ranch house door with a look of concern on his face.

"I vow to you, Marsh, that there was a light inside. I saw its flicker, small and dim, like a candle. But there was a light. Someone is here!"

"I saw no light, Juan. I think this house is empty. It feels empty to me, you know what I mean?"

"He may be in there."

"Yes, or there may be some terrified rancher in there with a rifle aimed at the door, waiting for us to come in. He probably figures Henry Kidd is paying a call."

"I'm going inside, Marsh."

Marsh sighed. "I know. I guess we have to."

"You need not, if you don't want. I can go in alone. It's my instinct, and not yours, that I am following."

"We're together in this. Try the door. If it's open, we'll both go in."

The door was indeed open, but the latch had an odd, unworking feel to it, as if the door had been forced and the latch damaged in the process.

Marsh and Carlos looked at each other. Carlos hefted up his rifle a little, and Marsh drew out his pistol, the only weapon he had left since he'd lost his rifle. Only the leather tie-down strap had kept him from losing the pistol when he plunged into the pit during his fight with Starky.

"All right, amigo . . . one, two . . . *three*!"

They lunged inside, weapons waving about. All they found was a dark and empty room.

"I guess nobody's here," Marsh said softly.

"I don't know . . . I have a feeling . . ."

"Let's look in the back."

"Wait."

Carlos found a lamp and lit it. With his rifle gripped in one hand and the lamp aloft, he advanced to the back, with Marsh just behind him.

"Look," Marsh said, pointing at the bed.

Very clearly there was a body lying there, with the cover pulled across the face. The partners glanced at each other.

"Kidd?" Marsh whispered.

"Starky Kidd doesn't put covers tidily across

his victims. He displays their bodies in terrible ways." Carlos reached over and gently lowered the cover, revealing the dead face of Ned Stevenson.

"No marks on the body," Marsh said.

"Yes. This was a natural death. But for some reason, whoever else lives in this house is now gone."

There was, however, one more door, one more room beyond it. Marsh gestured toward it.

Carlos moved that way, and sat the lamp on the floor far enough back so that it would not be tilted when the door opened. He grasped the knob and opened the door.

Light spilled in on the man standing just on the other side, with Marsh's revolving rifle upraised. Starky fired before Carlos could react. The bullet passed through Carlos's extended forearm, making him drop the rifle from suddenly limp fingers.

Marsh moved, raising his pistol, but Starky was faster. He was on Carlos in a moment, grabbing him, turning him, jamming the muzzle of the rifle up under his chin.

"No, sir, mister manhunter. You drop that pistol right now, or I blow off his head. Lay it down and kick it to the corner there."

Marsh knew Kidd. He knew that he would probably blow off Carlos's head anyway. But he had no option but to comply. He slowly lowered the pistol to the floor and left it there. He kicked it away as Starky had ordered.

In the glint of the lamplight, though, he noticed the shotgun that hung above a small fireplace to his left. Loaded? No way to know.

Starky grinned at him. "Good boy. How the hell did you get out of that pit? Never mind . . . you're dead for sure this time. Time for a little pleasure . . . time to watch your friend die, with you to follow!"

Carlos moved quickly, with no warning, pulling his head down and jamming the elbow of his good arm into Starky's gut at the same time. Starky grunted; the rifle fired, but the muzzle had been deflected and the bullet went out through the ceiling and roof.

Carlos pulled free and reached for his pistol. Marsh, meanwhile, went for the shotgun on the wall. His own pistol was out of sight and there was no time to grope for it in that dark corner.

Starky fired just a little more quickly than Carlos. The slug passed through Carlos's belly and snipped his spine. He fell like a sack of oats, dropping his pistol.

Marsh yanked the shotgun down, pulled back the hammers, turned toward Kidd.

Starky had the rifle aimed right at him. He pulled the trigger.

A dead click. For only the second time in Marsh's experience, the rifle had misfired.

Indeed the shotgun was loaded. Its roar was like a cannon in the enclosed room. The shot blasted out, caught Starky's right arm just below the wrist, and blew his hand off. The rifle, though, was in his left hand at that moment, and he did not lose it.

Starky let out a horrible wail, glared at his bleeding stump, then turned and plunged out through a window, shattering the glass. Marsh heard him come to his feet and run off into the night.

He would not pursue. There was Carlos to deal with.

He knelt beside the wounded man. "Juan . . . I'll find you help, Juan. I promise."

Carlos looked up at him. He smiled faintly. "I was not at my best tonight. In a better time I would have had him."

"No doubt."

"I must go now. . . . This is your quest alone from here out."

"No, Carlos. We'll get you help. You'll live."

"I'm afraid . . . it is too late . . . to harbor that hope . . . pray for me . . . pray for my soul . . . and when you do kill Starky Kidd, do it in my name . . . along with all the others . . . he has . . . murdered . . ."

Carlos went limp, his brown eyes no longer seeing, his lungs no longer drawing in air.

CHAPTER TWENTY-SEVEN

In a room in the only hotel in Woodhawk, Marian Stevenson looked out the window and watched the crowds gathering outside the sheriff's office fronting the jail. She shook her head.

Despite all that Ben had told her, she still could not reconcile the gentle Henry Kidd she had met with the brutal killer Ben described. Yet all the rest of the world seemed certain that Henry was a murderer and mangler. How could it be?

Like so much tonight, it all seemed unreal and impossible to understand. She pulled up a chair at the window and sat down, still watching the crowd, and wondering how long it would be before demands began being made for the sheriff to turn Henry over to them for immediate justice.

One sheriff, two deputies . . . and a crowd of at least sixty angry men, armed, ready to have a hanging before the sun came up. How long would the sheriff resist? And if he did resist, how could he possibly prevail?

She prayed for Henry. He simply could not be what they claimed. She imagined him huddling, terrified, back inside that dark jail, locked in a cell. It was for his sake that she had come here, leaving Ned's poor corpse there alone in the house. But what did it matter? Ned was gone, his body only an empty dwelling in which he used to live. But Henry was still alive.

Not for long, though, if what was happening outside progressed.

Marian stood. She was going down there. She would stand on that porch and face the crowd of lynchmen, and tell them that they had the wrong man. If there was a Henry Kidd who committed murder, it was not the same man now in the cell.

They would not believe her. She would not be able to stop them any more than the sheriff could. But it was her duty to make a stand no matter what the outcome.

She walked out of the hotel and toward the crowd, pushing her way in and through, making a path to the porch where the sheriff stood alone, shotgun in hand and a look of defiance thrown across his face like a mask that tried, vainly, to cover the face of fear beneath it.

*   *   *

An hour later, Marsh rode slowly into the edge of Woodhawk. Carlos's body was draped across his horse and tied in place. It seemed an ignoble way to carry the body of a friend and partner, but he had not been willing to leave him there in his blood, on the spot that such rubbish as Starky Kidd had killed him.

He hoped Starky was out there on the plains, bleeding to death from that stumped forearm. He hoped he died slowly, and hard, and that wolves and vermin mangled his body like he mangled so many he had killed.

Marsh stopped when he saw the crowd at the jail. He studied it, identified it as looking for all the world like a lynch mob, then rode forward. He thought better of it, though, and paused long enough to lead the horse bearing Carlos's body back into an alley. Riding up with a dead man just now might generate more confusion than it was worth, and he wanted to have a clear idea of what was going on here.

It surely had to do with Kidd. Right now in these parts, everything had to do with Kidd.

He dismounted and walked to the edge of the crowd. An eager boy of about thirteen was bobbing up and down, trying to see a little better what was going on.

"What's this all about?" Marsh asked him.

"They got him! They got Henry Kidd the murderer in that jail! And all these men here are ready to take him out and hang him!"

From the porch came a woman's voice, drawing Marsh's attention.

"I tell you, this is not the right man!" she said. "This is a gentle man, weak of mind but kindly and sweet. . . . He cried like a child over an injured dog as it died. In fact, a child is what he is in his mind! He's no killer!"

Marsh knew right away that they had Henry Kidd in there—not the murdering, falsely identified Henry Kidd who was really Starky, but the true Henry Kidd, the innocent.

"Move out of the way, Mrs. Stevenson!" someone demanded. "There's no call for you to involve yourself in this. Go back home and care for your husband!"

"My husband died tonight . . . and Henry Kidd tried to save him. He is no killer! Please, go home and don't do this lawless thing you're doing!"

"She's right," the sheriff said. "This is a clear violation of the law, and if you harm or kill the man in my custody, I know every one of you and will see you prosecuted for it!"

"Will you prosecute the whole county, Sheriff? Because the whole county is behind us! Hell, half the men in the county are here!"

That was quite an exaggeration, but the basic point was strong. The sheriff was bluffing, and everyone knew it.

The crowd surged then, moving in and up, closing in on the porch. The sheriff raised his weapon and the surge stopped, but clearly the next time it would go on through.

Marsh knew what he had to do. He began pushing through the densely packed crowd, toward the front. He sensed another surge, the final one, about to take place, so when he was only halfway through the crowd, he shouted, "Wait! Wait! I have something you need to see!"

Men glared at him, an upstart intruder interfering with their business, but he persisted and at last made it through to the porch. He stood there, a leather pouch he'd found in the ranch house slung across his shoulder. Marian looked at it, recognized it.

"That's my Ned's hunting pouch," she said softly, confused.

"Do you live in a ranch house with a man lying dead on the bed in the back?"

"Yes."

"Then I guess it is your Ned's pouch. I'll explain it all later." Then he turned to the crowd. "Tell me something: Does anyone here know about the scar on the hand of the murderer Kidd?"

"I've heard of it!" a man called back. Others echoed.

"Well, the story is true," Marsh said. "There is a scar on his right hand. And the man inside the jail, I'm willing to bet, has no scar. Right, Sheriff?"

"There is no scar," the sheriff confirmed.

"Are you saying that the man in the jail isn't Henry Kidd?" someone called.

"I'm saying that the man in the cell is not guilty of any murders. His name indeed is Henry Kidd, but he has a brother, named Starky, who has committed all the crimes.

Starky Kidd is an evil man, and he leaves the name of his half-wit brother at the scenes of the crimes so that he will take the blame instead of Starky himself! It's his scheme, and it must be a good one, because you men are just about to fall for it! If you lynch Henry Kidd, you've lynched an innocent man. The real killer, Starky Kidd, is still out there—and in much worse shape than he was earlier tonight, because I shot off his hand."

That brought a stunned reaction from the crowd.

"You're a liar!" someone shouted.

Marsh reached inside the leather pouch and brought out the shot-off hand of Starky Kidd.

"Bring that torch up here," he directed a torch-bearing man at the front edge of the crowd.

The torchlight revealed it clearly: On the back of the bloody, ugly hand was a jagged, very visible scar.

CHAPTER TWENTY-EIGHT

Corinne Serandon sat beside the creek, in the place she went when she was sad, staring into the water and wondering why she could not cry. Her father was dead! Murdered! Her sadness was deep, but she was unable to vent it. It festered in her, painful somewhere deep in her chest, and she wished she could turn back the clock and tell her father not to ride out with that absurd "army" that the preacher had pulled together. If only he'd stayed at the camp! He would be with her now. Her mother would not be alone in her room, her face buried in her pillow and the space beside her on the bed vacant.

Her mother could cry, and Corinne had at the beginning. Then sorrow had been overwhelmed by anger and the tears had stopped. The anger was at her father for having ridden out with the preacher's foolish army, for having not come back when the rest of them did, and for getting himself killed when his family needed him so badly. She was angry at the young man whom her father had died trying to save. She was angry at the Reverend Cacey for having drummed up the idea of a citizen army, anyway. She was even angry at God.

Most of all, she was angry at the murderer Kidd. A man who killed for no reason other than his own wicked mind. A man who stole away life, the best possession of all, and left girls without fathers.

It was deep night. The house, visible through the brush from where she was, was full of relatives and friends, sleeping on couches, spare beds, cots, blankets on the floor. It was that way when people died; all their loved ones piled in to make the grief easier to bear.

For Corinne, however, it had all seemed stifling. She had waited impatiently until the others slept, then she'd crept out here in the darkness to her secret place.

She had come to cry. So far, there had been no tears. Just anger, interspersed with periods of astonishing numbness.

It was hard to imagine how she and her mother would go on.

Then, from somewhere inside, a wall broke and her eyes filled. Seated on the ground, her knees up and her arms folded around them, she bowed her head and wept into her sleeves.

The pain was intense, the bitterness deep, but the tears softened them both. She cried for a long time—then raised her head sharply and suddenly.

She had just heard something behind her.

Corinne stood and turned. She saw no one, but her conviction that she was not alone was strong. "Hello?" she said.

No reply.

"Hello?" she said again. She began to suspect it was her uncle Martin. He was the kind to sneak about in silence—he made her uncomfortable very frequently.

The form emerged from the darkness, silhouetted dimly against the house. It was indeed her uncle.

"Uncle Martin? What are you doing out here?"

The figure moved, and Corinne drew in her breath sharply. It wasn't Uncle Martin! This man had only one hand. She could see only a stump where the other hand should be. There was a cloth of some sort tied over it, bound tightly with a strip of cloth.

"Who are you?" Corinne asked. She stepped back toward the creek.

"Hello, miss," the man said. He spoke softly and with no sound of threat. He sounded rather weak. "Miss, I am in need of help. I've had a terrible accident."

"Your . . . your hand?"

"Yes."

"You need a doctor, then."

"Maybe I do. But I can't go to one." He paused. "There's folks after me."

She hesitated, and a dreadful possibility arose in her mind. She backed away another step.

"I need somebody with me . . . so they'll leave me alone."

God help her, it was Kidd! It had to be—and what he was talking about was hostage-taking.

She backed away to the very edge of the creek and was about to scream, but with his good arm he raised a rifle. "No, miss. No. You just keep it quiet. You scream, you're dead. You understand me?"

Corinne looked longingly at the house that earlier she had so wanted to escape. Now she wished she'd never left it.

"Please . . ." she begged. "Please don't do this!"

"I got to do it, miss. Every son of a bitch in the country is after me. I'll never live unless I got somebody who they're afraid I'll hurt."

"If you take me, they'll try even harder to find you."

"They're going to try hard anyway. Now, come on. Keep your mouth shut and move."

She could tell from his voice that he was in pain. Her mind raced, looking for a ploy. "There's whiskey in the house," she said. "I can get it for you, to make you not hurt."

"Hell, no. I know what you're up to. I'll get whiskey later, somewhere else but here."

He was scared. She took note of it. This man

was terrified, and that made him all the more dangerous. But it might also make him careless, and give her an advantage.

This is the man who killed my father. The thought was overwhelming, hard to wrap her hand around. *This is the murderer who killed my father and threw him into a pit*.

Despite her terror, despite the fact that her knees quaked so much she feared she would fall and her hands trembled like aspen leaves, she vowed right then that he would not kill her too. No matter what, she would not let that happen.

No, she would kill him instead.

"Move!" he ordered again, in a sharp whisper.

She toyed once more with the idea of screaming. There were a houseful of people within earshot. They would be outside in a moment and Kidd would have no chance.

But she knew that they would find her dead. So she did not scream.

He approached her and nudged the gun into her back.

"Let's go, girl," he said. "Don't make me kill you. Because I will. Believe me, I will."

CHAPTER TWENTY-NINE

Marsh was growing hopeless. Part of it was pure exhaustion, and part of it was the fact that, once again, Starky Kidd had managed to evade capture. The night was his friend, not that of those who sought him. Marsh was beginning to wonder if he would make it away yet again— minus one hand, but still alive.

That lost hand, though, was the biggest source of hope for Marsh. If the bleeding was bad enough, Starky might already be dead out there somewhere in the darkness. If he had managed to stop the bleeding with a tourniquet, he might still feel compelled to seek medical help. That could expose him.

Part of Marsh hoped that Starky wasn't dead yet. If Starky was lying in some draw or in some hidden recess or cavern, his corpse might never be found. Marsh would be left with no way of knowing whether his quest was finished or not.

Marsh's quest aside, though, it would be best for the world if Starky Kidd had already left the mortal veil. Hell could have him, and innocent people could rest more easily in their beds.

They had reached the Stevenson spread and continued from there, searching in a widening swath all around in hope of finding Kidd either dead or dying from loss of blood. No luck. Reassembling, they had tried again, this time with different searchers going in different directions. Again there was no luck, but one man, by torchlight, did find a strip of bloodied cloth on the ground, about a hundred yards from the ranch house.

Kidd had made himself a bandage or tourniquet, it appeared. That indicated a certain state of ability and presence of mind despite the loss of his hand. Hope of finding him dead right away dwindled.

Discussion had followed. There was general agreement that Kidd was probably trying to cover a lot of ground under the veil of darkness. In his physical condition, thouugh, he probably would be attracted to settled areas, outlying ranches like the Stevensons' was, where he could find better bandaging, maybe something to purify his wound.

"Or a hostage," Marsh suggested.

The words laid a cold pall over the entire body of manhunters. It made sense. Kidd was alone now, fleeing, and if found would have no way to protect himself, unless he had another person he could threaten.

"I have a suggestion," the sheriff said. "I refuse to sit here and wait until daylight. Let's continue on to the Serandon spread. It's the closest one to this one. If there were lights visible, as well there might be given the bereavement there and the houseful of people that brings about, Kidd might have been attracted. It can't hurt to look. We may chance even to stumble upon his body between here and there."

It seemed as good a plan as anyone could come up with. Marsh pulled together his last fragments of strength and rode out with the determined band.

They were within sight of the Serandon ranch when the sheriff raised a hand and brought the band to a halt.

He did not have to tell what he had seen, because they all saw him now: a man riding pell-mell in their direction, frantic and fast.

"Kidd?" someone asked as rifles began to go up.

"I don't know—hold your fire until we are sure," the sheriff replied.

"That ain't Kidd," Marsh said. "I can see his hands, and he's got both of them."

"It's Michael Buckwood," said Port Bailey, who was among the manhunters.

"Ain't he Serandon's brother-in-law?" the sheriff asked.

"He is."

"What's he doing out like this at this hour?"

Buckwood thundered up and reined to a halt. "Sheriff, thank God you heard! How did you know?"

"Know what?"

"She's been took!"

"Who?"

"Corinne! My niece! She's gone, and we believe she's been took!"

The sheriff looked at Marsh. "Kidd," he said.

Marsh merely nodded, and felt he might become ill right where he was.

Marsh could not bear to look at the weeping widow Serandon. A husband lost, and now a daughter mysteriously vanished. It was clear from the tracks around the nearby creekside that she had been there, and that a man had been there as well. The torchlight had revealed some blood, too, indicating that the man was wounded. Not much blood, but not much would be expected if Kidd had applied a tourniquet.

"Where would Kidd go from here?" the sheriff mused aloud. "He knows that he is pursued—the fact he has taken a hostage shows that he is afraid and anticipates being caught."

"How well does Kidd know the country here?" Marsh asked.

"Fairly well, I believe," the sheriff replied. "I've heard it said that he came up into Texas some during the years he was in Mexico, and that he even killed a couple of people during that time. He would have had opportunity to get to know the terrain."

"Where would you go if you were on the run?" Marsh asked.

The sheriff paused, then said, "To the old McCade ranch. It's empty since McCade died . . . since he was murdered, I should note. He is one of those they say Kidd might have killed."

"Then let's go there."

"Let's do."

CHAPTER THIRTY

The fear was still there, but the anger was stronger. Her hatred of the man who had taken her—the man who had murdered her father—now coursed through her like the blood in her veins.

She tried but failed to not cry out when he slammed her onto the floor of the loft of the empty barn. Her hands were tied behind her, but not too tightly, because a man with one hand had no advantage when it came to tying knots. She had clenched her hands tightly when he tied her, and the ropes would be slippable . . . she hoped.

Her breath was knocked from her when she struck the loft floor; her eyes filled with grit and the dust of straw. She grimaced and lay still, for she had learned that any sort of unanticipated movement was always interpreted by Kidd as resistance, making him curse her and hit her.

"You just lie there, pretty thing," he said. He'd been calling her "pretty thing" for the last hour, which worried her. But when she'd realized how hurt he was, how much in pain and exhaustion, she ceased to worry that he might misuse her. He simply wouldn't have the strength.

"Sit up, you," he said. "Why you lying there?"

She sat up and looked around.

"You know this place?" he asked her.

"Yes," she said.

"I know it too. I come here quite a few years ago. Had to deal with a fellow who give me some trouble. Deal with him I did. They found him lying about a hundred feet in that direction . . . and that direction . . . and that direction . . ." Kidd laughed.

"You cut him in pieces," Corinne said.

"Yep."

"Why?"

"It's just what I do."

"Why do you kill?"

"Because . . . well, I don't know a man needs a reason to do what's in his nature. I kill because I hate the damned old world and because it hates me. I kill because . . . because I *like* it."

"You killed my father."

He looked at her in surprise. "I did?"

"You killed him and threw him into a pit in the hills. The ones who brought him back told about it."

"Hah! That was your father? I'll be damned!"

She was so full of hate at this moment that words failed her. She quietly and unnoticeably began working at the poorly tied bonds around her wrists. The moon was out now, spilling into the barn, and she was able to watch him with ease, and quit her wrigglings when he might notice them.

"I'll say one thing for your father: He fought hard. Surely did. He come out of the dark and fought me like a mad dog, that old fool did. But it was his mistake. I snapped his throat." He leaned over suddenly and raised his arms, making a claw shape with his one hand. "Ka-snap!" he said, and laughed.

But as he looked down at his stump, the laughter died. He shook his head and gnawed on his bottom lip a minute. "Damn him!" he said. "Damn him for shooting off my hand!"

She gave a little tug; one of the bonds came loose. She looked around, and in the moonlight noted that unusual rifle, lying on its side across the loft. She didn't know if it was loaded, or if so, in how many chambers—but there was a use she could make of it, loaded or not.

"They'll find you, you know," she said. "They're determined to find you and stop you."

He laughed. "Hell with them! You know how many folks have tried to get me? Hundreds of them! Know how many have caught me? Not a one! Not a damn one!"

"This time they will. My kin won't let you take me."

He lunged toward her, kneeling and shoving his ugly face close to hers. "Take you, you say? Girl, if it wasn't for the pain I'm in, if it wasn't for having to keep my eye and ear out in case them bastards come looking here." He paused, and his face grew more menacing. "If they do come . . . you let out one peep, and I'll put a knife through your throat, slow and rough, so it hurts like nothing you ever nightmared of . . . and you'll die slow, girl, and in pain."

She almost spat on him, but instinct warned her off.

Her hands were free. Her opportunity would come.

He backed away, then sat back against a post of the barn, about ten feet from her. He studied his stump in the moonlight.

"God, it hurts," he said. "Hurts so bad."

She said nothing. He stared at the stump, and for a long time said nothing, and in fact did not move. She began to suspect he was asleep, but his eyes remained open, blinking from time to time, staring at the stump. He remained that way for almost an hour, in that odd, waking sleep—but every time she began to move, his eyes shot up and glared at her in the moonlight.

She looked away, at the rifle on the floor. Her hands, free now, were gripped together behind her. She could move, lunge for that rifle. . . . She tried to calculate how long it would take to reach it, how quickly he would react.

He moved. Broke out of that strange stupor and came to his knees, staring out the open door of the loft to the dark but moonlit land beyond.

Riders. She heard them too now.

And she moved. She came to her feet and moved toward that rifle, getting her hands on it before Starky Kidd could even turn. He pivoted, glared at her in shock, and saw the rifle butt coming like a battering ram toward his face.

He threw up his hand to block it—but habit made him throw up the right arm rather than the left. There was no hand there, only a crusted, painful stump, and the rifle butt hit it hard, knocking loose the cloth tourniquet and making him scream in agony. He staggered back, tripped, and almost fell out of the window, his upper body actually passing out backward through the opening. There were a couple of old ropes hanging there, however, and his left hand managed to grab one of them and hang on. He tried to pull himself back inside.

She lifted the rifle, pulled the trigger. Either the gun was empty or it misfired, because nothing happened. He was almost back in again, and the riders were now actually visible out there on the plains, coming in like phantoms in the moonlight.

She pulled the trigger again, and again nothing happened.

He made it back in. She panicked, but only for a second. Turning the butt of the gun toward him again, she pushed forward with it and caught him in the forehead, hard. He fell back again, teetering on the edge of the window. He grabbed at the rope again, but this time missed it. She hit him again and he fell out of the window completely, hanging on by his one hand to the window's lower edge, his body swinging and dangling.

A dark inspiration struck her. She leaned out over him, grabbing the rope he had tried to save himself with. She looped it around his neck as he swatted at her with his handless stump. She looped it hard and tight, and tied it.

The riders were coming in close. She called to them. "I'm here! I'm here!"

Kidd cursed and roared at her, his hand beginning to slip. . . .

She had dropped the rifle at her feet, but now she picked it up again. She pounded his fingers with the butt of it, again and again, until at last he lost his grip and swung out, hanging by the neck above the barn door, choking, kicking . . .

The riders saw him, and watched in silence as he swung and flailed.

"Let's show a bit of mercy," the sheriff said. He pulled his rifle from its boot and raised it. Others saw and did the same.

"Out of the loft, Corinne!" a man yelled. "Come down now!"

She vanished from the window, and a couple of moments later was running out beneath Starky Kidd's kicking feet, racing toward the riders and safety.

"Ready . . . aim . . ."

The volley was deafening, and almost every shot struck the swinging target. Starky Kidd was hammered by scores of bullets, his body destroyed in less than a second, his miserable life shot out of him. One of the bullets missed him, though, and struck the rope, clipping it almost completely. Kidd swung dead a few seconds, then the rope snapped and his corpse fell with a thud at the barn door.

No one spoke for almost half a minute. The sheriff rebooted his rifle.

"Well, folks, I guess that's that," he said.

Epilogue

"It really didn't come out like I thought it would," Marsh Perkins said to the widow Serandon. He'd talked with her, and with Corinne, and told them of his sorrow that their loss had come, indirectly at least, because of him. And they had forgiven him. That was easier now that Starky Kidd was gone. Forgiveness, peace of mind, hope—they all came easier now that the demon was dead. "It really wasn't what I thought it would be at all," he went on. "My grandmother had a vision that showed me killing Kidd."

"In a way, you did," she said. Having heard his story, she was impressed by the dedication with which he had searched for the killer. "If not for your pursuit and persistence, Kidd might not have been finally stopped."

"I'm just glad it's over. But sorry it came at the cost of lives. Good people . . . Juan Carlos. Mr. Serandon. All the ones murdered."

"What will become of Henry Kidd?" Corinne asked.

"The widow Stevenson, a fine woman, is taking him in. He'll work for her, live in her home. For the first time in his life, he'll have a good situation. It's good. He's an innocent soul, as innocent as his brother was wicked. I hope no one will hold against him the sins of his brother."

"And what will become of you now, Marsh?" Mrs. Serandon asked.

"I'm going home," Marsh said. "I've seen done what I was sent to do. I even have the hand of Henry Kidd to bring back, as I was told to do. I'm eager to get there. It will be good to be home again."

"You will come back someday?"

He couldn't help but cast a glance at Corinne.

"I'll come back someday," he said. "You can be sure of it."

WILL CADE

Larimont

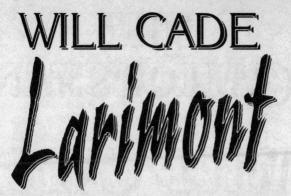

John Kendall doesn't want to go back home to Larimont, Montana. He has to—to investigate the death of his father. At first everyone believed that Bill Kendall died in a tragic fire… until an autopsy reveals a bullet hole in Bill's head. But why is the local marshal keeping it a secret? John isn't quite sure, so he sets out to find the truth for himself. But the more he looks into his father's death, the more secrets he uncovers—and the more resistance he meets. It seems there are a whole lot of folks who don't want John nosing around, folks with a whole lot to lose if the truth comes out. But John won't stop until he digs up the last secret. Even if it is one better left buried.

___4618-0 $4.50 US/$5.50 CAN

THE GALLOWSMAN

WILL CADE

Ben Woolard is a man ready to start over. The life he's leaving behind is filled with ghosts and pain. He lost his wife and children, and his career as a Union spy during the war still doesn't sit quite right with him, even if the man sent to the gallows by his testimony was a murderer. But now Ben's finally sobered up, moved west to Colorado, and put the past behind him. But sometimes the past just won't stay buried. And, as Ben learns when folks start telling him that the man he saw hanged is alive and in town—sometimes those ghosts come back.

___4452-8 $4.50 US/$5.50 CAN

DOUBLE EAGLES
ANDREW J. FENADY

Captain Thomas Gunnison has been entrusted with an extremely vital cargo. His commerce ship, the *Phantom Hope*, is laden with two thousand Henry rifles, weapons that could turn the tide of victory for the Union. Even more important, though, is fifteen million dollars in newly minted double eagles, money the Union needs to finance the war effort. So when the *Phantom Hope* is attacked and crippled, Gunnison makes the only possible decision—he and his men will transport the gold across the rugged landscape of Mexico, to Vera Cruz. Gunnison's caravan could change the course of history . . . if bloodthirsty Mexican guerrillas and Rebel soldiers don't stop it first!
